BLUE CONDOR

What if you could control the weather?

A gripping conspiracy thriller from

MARTIN & MARTIN

ACKNOWLEDGEMENTS FROM THE AUTHOR
Loren Dale Martin, BS, JD (1940-2017)

Dedicated to the memory of my friend, Gary Towers.

For my family: Marilyn Monson Martin,
Robert Loren, David Dale, Thomas Spencer, Richard
Leno, Holly Lynn, Melanie Jane, Laurie Ellen.
Families are forever.

ACKNOWLEDGEMENTS FROM THE CO-AUTHOR
Robert Loren Martin, BS, MPC

For my father.

Dedicated to all those who serve honorably.

SYNOPSIS

Years of top-secret government experiments in modification of the world's weather systems has resulted in increasingly violent storms and "natural" disasters on a global scale. Victor Sine, Chief of Security, receives information causing him to believe his entire weather control project may be compromised by the intentional or unintentional actions of John Wayment, a popular TV personality in Denver, Colorado. National security requires he be stopped, bought off, or otherwise compromised.

Frustrated by normal channels, Sine engages an old Mafia contact in Kansas City to gather information on Wayment. His home is broken into and his best friend mysteriously dies in a military helicopter accident. Sine's frustration continues to grow through the deliberately modified eruption of Mount St. Helens. Finally, being unable to control Wayment, Sine orders a contract on his life.

Loren Martin loved to create, write, and teach. During our remarkable lifetime together he created books, businesses, backyards, family vacations, political campaigns, and many other adventures that we shared through more than fifty years of marriage. We have been incredibly blessed with seven children and thirty-four grandchildren.

He was always and is forever my eternal companion and best friend. In his honor I hope you will thoroughly enjoy this tense and gripping tale full of intrigue, deception, and enduring faithfulness to a dream, which he first envisioned more than forty years ago.

-Marilyn Monson Martin, 2018

Loren and Marilyn Martin photos: ©1967 from the Martin Family archive, and ©2010 by Robert Taylor Photography, www.roberttaylorphotography.com, used with permission.

Martin Family photo ©2013 by Elle Photos, www.ellephotos.com, used with permission.

This work of fiction was conceived, researched, and drafted by my father in the early 1980s. I was a teenager at the time he finished the initial draft. He'd given me a typed copy in a three-ring binder, saying it needed work, but here was a dramatic story that deserved to be told. The document was stored and later rediscovered after his death on June 28, 2017, from complications of Alzheimer's disease. He was seventy-six years old.

Following his death, I read through the draft again with all his old news clippings and notes. Its key subject matter of sweeping climate change and subversive weather modification are even more hotly relevant today! I knew I had to complete this novel and get it published as a tribute to his extraordinary life. Everyone loves a good conspiracy and murder-plot story, and there's always media buzz on extreme weather, increasing nor'easters, late-season storms, global warming, earthquakes, or the latest volcanic eruption.

My father's government and law experience during the 1960s and '70s included direct contact with people who were actively engaged in weather modification projects and research, including the use of explosives. Descriptions and personality profiles depicted are based on actual situations and experiences he'd witnessed first-hand while involved with various military and government projects and also while investigating Mafia and organized crime activities.

My father was a brilliant and passionate man who cared deeply about people. He was driven by a personal heartfelt duty to protect and to serve and to uphold the law. He went to law school at the University of Utah and primarily spent his career as a practicing attorney in Utah, including a term as Davis County Attorney, just north of Salt Lake City. Before this he was an FBI Special Agent and military officer. He was stationed with the U.S. Army Signal Corps at NATO HQ in Germany during the late 1960s, when I was a young boy, then during the early 1970s he was assigned to FBI field offices in Oklahoma and Kansas. He was also a lay clergyman, politician, cancer survivor, businessman, and most importantly to him, a family man.

August Veraart of Holland, Tor Bergeron of Sweden, and Germany's Walter Findeisen were well known pioneers in the science of weather modification. Descriptions and dialogue related to them herein are fictitious, but the work they did in the 1930s is not. Lord Byron, Mary Shelly, Mark Twain, Charles Warner, Fidel Castro, Fulgencio Batista, Benjamin Franklin, Adolf Hitler, Heinrich Himmler, Richard Nixon, Jimmy Carter, Ronald Reagan, Sheikh Mujibur Rahman, Anwar Sadat and KWGN-TV are mentioned only for their historical reference.

All other named characters are fictitious with the exception of Chun Byung-in, Sohn Dong-hui, and Vasiliy Kazmin. Radio communications of Vasiliy Kazmin are taken from transcripts of the actual record, which were kept secret until 1993. The Soviet Union eventually admitted to deliberately shooting down KE007 on September 1, 1983, claiming it was on a MASINT spy mission (to gather measurement and signature intelligence). The incident provoked an extremely tense moment during the Cold War and conflicting reports about circumstances leading up to the event have never been fully resolved.

May these pages about the adventures and travails of John and Sharon Wayment provide an entertaining escape, as well as inspiration to never fear pursuing your own passions and dreams!

-Robert Loren Martin, 2018

Aboard the USS Midway in 2015 with my father Loren and Uncle Scott Monson, both veterans. Photo credit to my mother, Marilyn!

Anchorage, September 1, 1983

The night was crisp and clear as the 747 lifted smoothly from the Alaskan runway. Like a giant lumbering bird, the plane rose effortlessly toward the upper air currents, then turned slowly southwest as it glided along its predetermined flight path. A few wispy clouds hung like strings of cotton candy. Inside the plane it was big, comfortable, and warm. Flight attendants began to move about the cabin as the no smoking light went out. It would be a long flight. All seemed perfectly normal, everything routine.

Hana, a small, dark-haired six-year-old, was peering out one of the center port-side windows as the plane rose. She continued watching through the window, long after any ground lights had shrunk to pinpoints, having faded well into the distance.

On every flight, no matter how many pass into history, there are always some passengers who experience apprehension. Their overactive imaginations conjure up fears of disaster, anticipating the worst. They can get very nervous looking out of airplane windows, seeing nothing but blue sky and the fading world left behind.

As the blackness closed in around the plane, young Hana was one of those kinds of passengers. She was anxious and shaking inside. There was nothing left to see anymore outside the window. Everything was completely dark now, yet within her fledgling mind she couldn't shake the feeling that something was wrong. Her mother was sitting right there next to her. Surely there was nothing to worry about. Hana tried to calm herself by thinking back across the emptiness to remember again the touch of her grandfather's kiss before she'd left.

Grandpa gave great hugs and kisses. He'd made her feel warm and wanted. These memories helped Hana to not be so nervous, because she knew instinctively that she had a whole lifetime ahead of her, and Grandpa would be there to help her along. He had been there before. Grandpa made her feel like she would live forever.

When her mother had taken her by the hand to board the plane back to Korea, a slight tear had rolled down her cheek as they walked away together toward the airport terminal door and the big bird that would take her away from Grandpa.

Now, unseen in the vast darkness far below, lie only the unlimited expanse of the North Pacific. Its black surface was heaving, concealing mountains, valleys, and millions of years of evolution within its hidden oblivion.

Up in the first-class section, a Navy veteran nearly fifty years of age also gazed pensively out the window, keeping watch into the blackness. Visions of his recent report to Congress kept passing through his mind in review. Had he said all the right things? Had he said enough? He was determined to block Communist countries from financing their purchases of American agricultural commodities with tax dollars. "Federal money should never be used to assist commies," he mumbled silently to himself. Would they be able to muster the votes necessary to win passage within the current session? He feared his reputation depended on it.

The Congressman wasn't in a good mood. He was on his way to Seoul to celebrate an important anniversary with the South Korean government and to recognize recent victories in blocking the continued spread of communism, but there was so much more that needed to be done. He didn't particularly feel like traveling all this way only for celebrating work that wasn't done, but they needed to show respect to their political allies. Someone needed to be there for representation and to help keep the faith. Finally, he rested himself back, switched on the small reading lamp, and reached for the seat-back pocket to begin thumbing through the pages of Fortune.

Meanwhile, far back in coach, Hana finally rested her head down on the pillow at her mother's shoulder. Her mother draped a small blanket over her knees and smiled.

Steady now at cruising altitude, the pilot set and locked the automatic controls to a distant radio signal, miles ahead and far below. The pilots relaxed as science took over to carefully guide the craft along. Everything was in order. Nothing could go wrong.

Distance and hours passed as flight attendants completed duties, adjusted seats, and saw to every comfort and convenience for the 246 passengers onboard. The flight continued humming through the night, a giant of modern marvels, traveling peacefully and inexplicably further and further off-course toward the west.

The mundane of routine had settled in with nearly all of the passengers as their looming death began to rise on radar under the mask of the blackness. There was no warning before the first missile struck the plane, only a blinding flash of explosion, sudden spinning color from splattering blood, and the terror of screams as the fuselage ripped open. The massive plane shook, then faltered, then fell into a deep downward spiral as men, women, and children were violently torn apart mid-air. The melancholy strains of Cho Yong-pil's "The Woman Outside the Window" was still playing from the small stereo speakers in the aircraft's flight deck.

There were more explosions, still more immediately snuffed out screams, then a long still silence, followed by the gruesome far away noise from innumerable body and machine parts dropping down in chunks with heavy slapping sounds into a dark and watery grave.

Southern California, January 1959

John Wayment was the frustration of his third-grade class. He was never a problem child and Miss Wilson knew he was bright, but she just couldn't reach him no matter how hard she tried. His interest in the classroom simply flittered away.

She tried the usual and traditional things to capture his attention. She read fairy tales and told stories to inspire his imagination. She asked him to concentrate carefully and draw what he was feeling during finger painting, but John only made a few quick blue-gray strokes and said they were clouds. All he wanted was to be outside, watching for airplanes, animals, goblins, and monsters in the sky.

Her breakthrough came one Friday morning in late January. John was acting very excited and could hardly sit still. At recess he didn't go outside. He walked up to Miss Wilson's desk and started talking, first standing on one foot, then the other. This wasn't unusual, but this time he was really talking to her, not just talking out loud.

John talked first about his favorite things, the clouds, the wind, the trees, and how everything outside is connected, but then he went on. He talked about last night's weather forecast, about how things outside were different than predicted yesterday, how the bugs must be affected by the lower than usual temperatures, and something about all the ships at sea.

Then John said something important.

It wasn't really what John said, it was more the way he said it. It must have been the tone of his voice, or the tilt of his head, or the shuffle from one foot to the other. Whatever it was, it hit her like a revelation. John had simply looked at her and said slowly, in kind of a whisper, "Miss Wilson, don't you think it would be neat to tell the weather?" John's eyes then kind of dazzled for a second and that was it. He headed outside with the rest of the kids.

She thought about the encounter all through the weekend. What would she do with this revelation? Finally, she landed upon a thought.

Monday morning before class she rearranged a tack board and cleared a four-foot space on the wall. After talking briefly with John, she made the announcement, John Wayment would be the official third grade weather forecaster! "I'll bet he'll start with talking about the clouds," she thought as she smiled to herself.

******

Scott Watson lived three blocks from John, right near the school. Scott didn't want to be a weather forecaster, or a fireman, or an astronaut. He wanted stars on his shoulder and a jeep under his boots. He'd become an Army drill sergeant before age four. John and Scott had been friends forever. John knew he needed Scott to help plan his secret mission. The two waited anxiously one night until long after dark when they knew their parents would be asleep.

They wore their darkest clothing. The meeting place was on the south side of the school, behind a tall bush. Their secret password was "eagle."

Arriving within earshot of the bush John whistled like a bird twice. "Eagle," whispered back from the bush. John ran over and started babbling at the top of his voice. "Get down!" said the concealed whisper, "D'ya wanna blow this whole mission?" He dropped quickly down onto the grass and found himself suddenly staring at a nearly unrecognizable friend. Concealed way back underneath the bush, with thick black streaks of shoe polish on his face like a star NFL player, Scott was lying in the dirt hugging a rubber ball and a small wooden stick that looked sort of like a gun. John stopped talking immediately and crawled underneath the bush beside him. They whispered back and forth about their plan, and each carefully plotted step.

The fence on the south side of the cafeteria was steel posts and wooden slats. Creeping around the building to the north, John watched as Scott threw the ball that was tied to a long string up and over the roof. "Hold this," Scott said, handing him the end of the string. "Start pulling on it when you hear me whistle." Scott scurried around to the south side and opened his backpack. He attached the other end of the string to a thick knotted rope, then whistled three short bursts. John pulled on the string, now with the rope attached. Scott had secured the other end tightly to one of the steel posts. Black-faced Scott then appeared suddenly from around the corner, smiling widely. They both tested their weight by pulling hard on the knotted rope, then in turn they each scrambled up the wall to the top of the roof.

Two nails secured the base plate to the roof. The upright stick was fixed in place. Scott returned the small hammer to his backpack as John placed the hole in the crossbar over the nail. It was beautiful. No one knew about this and tomorrow absolutely everyone would notice what they'd done. They swore allegiance. "Friends are forever." They would never tell anyone how they'd accomplished this. Pride tickled their spines as they climbed back down from the cafeteria, removed the rope, and headed back to their homes.

It was a long night of waiting in anticipation.

The next morning John and Scott arrived at the school twenty minutes early. They stood side by side to gaze up at their clandestine achievement. The copper tail glistened in the sun as the light wind changed slightly from southeast to south. They had mounted the most magnificent weather vane ever!

It actually wasn't much, just a thin copper fin attached on the end of a long stick, but they had put it up there. John gave Scott a high-five. They watched the weather vane turn slightly with the wind rather than watching the Stars and Stripes being raised up the school flagpole by the sixth graders. John kept sneaking glances at the weather vane through the classroom window all day. If he stood on his toes near the window, he could just barely see the top. Who would notice their amazing achievement first?

No one noticed, not even Miss Wilson.

It was three weeks before anyone noticed, and this was only because a strong wind picked the stick right up off the nail and blew it with great force through Miss Myrtle's fourth grade window. Miss Myrtle was struck on the cheek by a piece of glass when the window imploded, and it drew blood. Scott thought her reaction was actually rather funny, but she didn't think so. "I could've lost my eye!"

Of course, there was an investigation conducted by the Principal.

With wisdom, John's father and Scott's father worked out a plan with the Principal. The boys would pay for the window and apologize to Miss Myrtle. The Principal decided a school weather vane was actually a good idea, and that the cross bar should be replaced. This time a steel ball was placed on top of the nail to keep the whole thing tightly together. Miss Myrtle was disgusted. "That piece of garbage that came through my window should be destroyed." She wanted her rightness to be known to the world. Nobody liked Miss Myrtle, the old battle-ax.

The experience got Scott thinking about how cool it might be if he could predict the weather for military maneuvers. His motivation was Myrtle, of course, since she didn't approve. She couldn't stop their dreams, though. The boys were now infamous!

Growing up in Southern California in the 1950s and '60s, John and Scott didn't just hope for clear weather days. They grew accustomed to expect them. Trapped in a microclimate without dramatic seasonal weather shifts, the boys jumped early into weather curiosity with a passion and vigor reflecting their personalities. John started tracking good weather and bad weather days with a smiley face or frowny face on his Amazing Stories calendar. Scott acquired an old radio receiver to listen late at night to the coded messages broadcast to the ships at sea, and also to the words of the National Weather Service.

The two friends grew up together, rode their bicycles together, then traded them up for used cars. By age seventeen John started giving a three-minute daily weather report at 4:30 PM on the local college radio station. He already knew for certain he was eventually going to be on television. This was never a question or a make-believe dream to John, it was simply a statement of fact. It was merely a matter of timing.

John predicted the stronger than normal spring runoff of sixty-nine. However, he did not predict how much water would really run-down Grant Street after the storm drain backed up. A massive river of water and debris poured down the street, breaking windows and washing away yards. Two houses were ruined and several others significantly damaged. He felt responsible. He felt an obligation to warn people.

Scott thought the floods were actually great fun and volunteered to help fill sandbags. He organized his own platoon of students from the high school ROTC. They claimed credit for saving a bridge which otherwise would've been washed out. Sticks had plugged the culvert on the north side and his team worked furiously to direct the water away until it could be cleared. They got their picture in the paper over the headline, "ROTC Fights Flood."

When he was packing up his car to leave for college Scott looked across the street at the elementary school. The little weather vane was still up there, perched atop the cafeteria. The copper piece had faded green, but the crossbar was still attached. He found Miss Myrtle's old classroom window, remembered back fondly to that secret night mission of so many years before, and smiled. Ha!

> *"It is the supreme art of the teacher to awaken*
> *joy in creative expression and knowledge."*
> —*Albert Einstein*

"Of course, the future is uncertain. This is probably why most people only seem to care about instant gratification," thought John, working on his home computer past midnight again in his basement office.

Weather forecasting is naturally ambiguous. No one can track the paths of distant weather patterns with any kind of precision. Projected more than one day, or even a few hours, and facts become fantasy. It is impossible to predict the weather long-term because of the chaotic nature of natural laws that govern the behavior of the elements and the atmosphere.

Sure, that was yesterday, but what about today? Today's world is one of satellites and radar maps and room-filling supercomputers. With all this burgeoning new technology it had to be possible to more accurately know and predict the weather many days, weeks, or perhaps even months or years in advance, didn't it?

John Wayment thought so.

John had grown up fascinated by the weather, but also by science fiction, mythology, and people who dreamed dreams foretelling the future. He was awed and inspired by the people who first imagined the possibilities of space travel and satellites, of radio and television, of near instantaneous wireless communications. Imagine sending electrical messages through the air, of connecting everyone together at the speed of light. That was pure fantasy yesterday.

John liked to think of himself as a radical weather nerd. These kinds of revolutionary thoughts always engaged him. He dreamt day and night of not only predicting the weather, but of having omniscient, god-like, meteorological supremacy. He dreamt of having geological dominance like Zeus of old!

A person who could control weather elements could change the world. That's why those elements have always been left to the Gods. Could natural elements — the weather — the source of disastrous earthquakes, tornados, and volcanoes, be enhanced, diminished, and controlled by man? For many years now, John had studied this question, worked it, and even slept it. If possible, he would have eaten it.

John was a romantic workaholic and weather control had become his relentless mistress, an enticement which insistently beckoned to him, but which could never be fully satisfied. So maybe he couldn't be like Zeus, but perhaps he might be like Prometheus, who could foresee events and give people warning.

Most people dwell only upon their most immediate concerns, worrying incessantly over doubts and fears, thinking nothing for their long-term future. They wallow in the perceived comforts of being told by someone else what to do and how to behave. They give all their service to "the man," meaning anyone who could be held responsible other than themselves.

John's personal beliefs, however, were pointedly juxtaposed with those. John was not most people. He genuinely cared for humanity and didn't much care about short-term comforts or being told what to do or how to behave. John's focus was consistently on the bigger picture and knowing deep down inside that anything was possible.

Recently John had been working himself to exhaustion. He'd been collecting extreme weather data from all over the world for the past several years. He'd compiled, evaluated, and reevaluated. He'd studied the devastating aftermaths of earthquakes, tsunamis, hurricanes, and volcanoes. He could see patterns of what he believed to be very real increasing threats, most significantly influenced by man's deliberate tampering with and attempted augmentation of natural climate conditions. Surely what he was finding was not completely natural.

He tiptoed upstairs into the bedroom and slipped down under the covers next to his sleeping wife, Sharon. John tried to lie still and relax, but his thoughts didn't want to stop. He found himself again and again just twisting and turning.

He tried counting sheep, then he tried counting coyotes coming to eat the sheep. He tried breathing deliberately and counting slowly each inhale and exhale: in and out, sluggishly, in and out. Was the world's weather really being modified in unnatural attempts for control? What else could be causing these distinctive jet stream patterns, wild atmospheric temperature fluctuations…and sharp increases in the number of his recurring deep and heavy breaths? Suddenly, he sat up in bed, frustrated.

"John, stop pulling at the covers!" whispered Sharon in uneasy semi-consciousness. "What time is it? You've been working way too much. Lie down and go back to sleep."

John lay back down, but his mind still insisted in racing on. Awake or asleep, good mythology flirts with the soul and sneaks in through cracks of reality to make itself real.

"Reality is really only what we choose it to be," interjected John's subconscious stubbornly. "Anything is possible, even modifying the weather, if you're not afraid of failure, that is." Everyone has dreams!

The sudden strike of the old grandfather clock in the hallway startled him. It bonged deeply once, then again.

"Get to sleep," he told himself sternly.

Other thoughts then flipped across his perception as his body drifted in and out of fitful slumber: what becomes our reality is determined and called forth by ourselves to ourselves. What becomes real is first conditioned in our mind, before being perceived by our senses. Therefore, our dreams actually become our reality, and our dreams can embolden either heaven or hell!

John's persistent need for philosophical over-analysis sometimes isolated him from the rest of the world. But maybe this was also the source of his frenetic insomnia and occasional nightmares? After all, if you know about impending doom and do nothing to stop it, are you not just as responsible for the tragic outcome as the source? Forthrightly, through your inaction you have thereby become part of the cause of the disaster because you knew yet chose to do nothing to prevent it from happening.

This kind of self-imposed weight of responsibility was not to be taken lightly. John knew just as soon as he could develop more reliable ways to track and predict severe weather he would be able to warn people in advance and save lives. He would be able to shout it from the rooftops. John loved an audience and craved a bigger audience. He knew if he could capture a growing audience long-term, if he could help them all better understand the weather, its potential, its power, its beauty and its majesty, then he had found his elusive shadow called "success."

A world of amazing weather stories was the world in which John reveled. He was determined to create his own reality. John had built a custom computer system in his basement, running his own numerical weather prediction models and simulation programs using primitive equations. He would be able to foretell future weather better than anyone else alive! He was unwavering in his goal.

Then, faintly amidst the cheering of the crowds within his happy dreamland, John heard all too soon the familiar gradually-increasing beeping of his alarm clock awakening on the nightstand. He slowly opened his eyes, swung out of bed, slapped the clock back into silence, and stumbled toward the shower. The hall clock bonged four times. He had two hours until airtime.

******

John arrived at the newsroom shortly after 5:30 AM with his coffee in hand. Everything there was already buzzing. Information was coming in twenty-four hours a day, seven days a week, from all over the world and being packaged up nicely into quick thirty-second announcements, because viewers' attention spans are short, of course.

"Watch us later today. Watch us tomorrow. We'll show you more tomorrow. We have the secret keys." The deliberately good-looking news anchors embody every television station's policy of being the definitive authority on what qualifies as news, on what's coming soon, on what's going to be relevant and important for the future.

Starting bright and early the actors in the studio put on their masks of self-expression to appeal to a piece of glass. With practice, these performers can capture their audience effortlessly and become the center of attention, while the huge supporting crew behind the scenes remain unseen. The audience is not supposed to know all the hidden details of how the show was so carefully prepared beforehand, the excitement subliminally shaped to come forth at precisely the defined times, of how the beautiful pictures are all orchestrated with carefully chosen words.

The presentations must all be perfect. Bad days are not allowed on live television, or fickle people will mock, and the all-important viewer ratings will begin to fall.

6:10 AM came far too quickly for John's comfort, but the sports announcer was obviously wide awake, nearly yelling, waving his arms madly. He was reading from the script of words that rolled before him, close to the camera. Engineering had prepared his cues. A red light indicated where he was to look for eye contact with unseen millions. He was appealing to his audience, working himself into excitement over the same things he'd read and tracked for years. This team won, and that team lost. This call was thoroughly unexpected, and that score was particularly spectacular. The presentation must always feel new. Excitement will close the sale to keep companies paying for advertising and to keep people from losing attention.

On television, success is promoted as something to be achieved later and recognized in anyone you are not. Advertising is carefully calculated so that feelings of inadequate sex sells toothpaste. Buy this product and be popular. Fear of failure or rejection sells coffee. Follow this path to capture fame and fortune. The story seems to always be the same.

Just two minutes now until John's airtime.

In two minutes, the magical Rocky Mountain weather forecaster would emerge onto the scene. Just off the set John stretched broadly, cracked his knuckles, and shook his head back and forth to get his blood pumping faster. He was expected to be able to fill the morning airwaves with words, clouds, and the thrill of thunder. The sorcerer was ready to step up into his workshop! He had his charts prepared and seven-day forecast ready. His lead-ins and final jokes had been practiced and memorized. It isn't easy to come up with 365 jokes and then begin a new year. The studio had writers assigned to this task.

One minute.

Like sports, forecasting weather is big business. Many things from energy-demand to crop yields vary widely based upon the weather. If it could be known that January's temperatures are going to be significantly colder than normal, investors may speculate and buy natural gas or heating oil futures. Conversely, if it could be known that January will be mild, investors might hedge. What if it were possible to know how many tons of commodities, soybeans, corn, wheat, and rye will be produced in Kansas next year? What about across the world? Commodity markets rise and fall upon speculation in futures and those markets fluctuate in millions a day.

John's dreams kept replaying in his mind. He knew by studying harder he should be able to predict the weather farther out beyond a standard seven-day forecast. He just knew it had to be possible. He didn't know when the dream first came. Perhaps it was always there within him. If he could predict the storms better than his competitors, he could share this with his audience. A person who knows the future can own the world!

Ten seconds.

As the final moments until show time ticked away John imagined he was already that person. He visualized living that dream as Rainmaker. His weather prediction was going to become the most reliable and most accurate in the world. He wanted to be able to tell people what's going to happen in India, Africa, China, and Russia next year. He wanted to be able to share when extra rain was going to provide stronger growth in the world's food supply and when drought was unavoidable.

Were there undiscovered patterns to it all? He knew there were. The motivation to predict the future had driven John Wayment's dreams for more than twenty years.

"Stand by." The floor director held up his hand, pointed to John, and ticked off his fingers, "Five, four, three, two, one."

The small light on camera two glowed red.

"All men dream: but not equally.
Those who dream by night in the dusty recesses
of their minds wake in the day to find that it was
vanity: but the dreamers of the day are
dangerous men, for they may act their dreams
with open eyes, to make it possible."

–T. E. Lawrence

In 1970, during John and Scott's freshman year at sunny UCLA, the Bhola tropical cyclone struck Bangladesh on the other side of the world. Peak winds reached 185 km/h (115 mph). More than 450,000 people died. It was not the most powerful cyclone. Other storms since then have been recorded with winds well over 260 km/h (160 mph). Yet Bhola is still considered the deadliest tropical cyclone on record. Nearly half a million people all dead and rotting in one place about the size of Iowa. It's hard to imagine.

Bangladesh has an extensive sea coastline and eighty percent of the land is in floodplain. It has been reported as the second poorest nation in the world. The numbers vary from time to time, but nobody seems to take much notice, or care. On average, more than 6,000 people die across the Ganges-Brahmaputra delta every year in storms and in floods. Devastating storms seem to come every few years in cycles. During 1987-1988, two thirds of the country was under water. This happened again in 1998. Bangladesh's population of 160 million people is also projected to grow by a further fifty million by 2050, putting more people routinely in harm's path.

Politically, perhaps only government agencies that collect money by reporting on morbidity and mortality take much notice about steadily increasing storm surges reported around the world. The cynical may wonder at how the money is collected to do such reporting. How much goes to data collection costs? Do the data collectors also become humanitarian relief?

Operating under the World Health Organization, many teams of physicians and medical technicians were sent consistently into Southern Asia during the mid-1970s in a concerted effort to help eradicate smallpox. In 1980, the World Health Assembly would officially declare the world free of this devastating disease. However, in 1970, that hadn't happened yet.

******

Zaynab bint-Ahmad and her small child were all that remained. The flood had washed away her other child and all her kin, along with their entire village built from dirt and grass. Zaynab's village was southwest of Faridpur, in the plain of the Ganges and Brahmaputra rivers, seventy-five miles from the expansive capital city of Dacca, the fourth most densely populated city in the world, often described as the Venice of the East with its elaborate palaces, gardens, tombs, and mosques.

Yet the capital city with all its riches and trade was foreign to her, as foreign as Mount Everest, just two hundred miles northwest. If it had been possible to see that far, Zaynab and her child would have been awed by the majesty and height of the wind-swept top. However, that high place where snow perpetually blows over the Himalayan range, was also as far away from Zaynab's reality as eternity was from the edge of the galaxy. To Zaynab her small village and simple existence was all of her reality.

Zaynab had followed her husband there, working someone else's land, but this was their home. She drew comfort from the feel of the warm mud paths connecting her with other local villages. They had farmed rice there, right up until this dreadful day when rice, soil, and family were washed away and replaced with disease and death. As the earthen and grass walls of the village began to crumble Zaynab thought perhaps this was an act of one of the thousands of Hindu Gods. Maybe the Gods had forgotten or didn't care. It really didn't matter, though. The result was disease and death, whether Muslim or Hindu.

Some years later there would be hope of rebuilding and of property ownership for the poor in this region. Sheikh Mujibur Rahman, with the support of Bengali forces, would leave exile in India and defeat the Pakistani forces to declare the existence of the independent nation of Bangladesh. Today, however, storms originating hundreds of miles from home over the Jamna River had collected with monsoon and cyclone effect to wipe the face of the earth. Water was seeping through and rushing over all the land, washing away the soil and crops to the sea, leaving little if anything left upon which to sustain life.

Zaynab waited for days until the water flow had stopped and the mud began to settle. She found herself alone, without home or food, with her six-month old boy, huddled with strangers for warmth. Zaynab cared for her child by nursing as she wandered. She thought about going somewhere else to live, but there was no place else to go.

After three weeks Zaynab's milk dried up. She noticed small red marks on the baby's body, and he felt feverish. What had gone wrong? Why was there no warning, no time to prepare? How was it possible to find food now for seventy-four million people, or even twenty million?

It wasn't just the flood washing away villages and killing by drowning that was the biggest tragedy. It was the aftermath. There was a waste of desolation as humans ravaged in a desperate attempt to survive. The long lines of displaced people mingled across the dust plains as far as the blurred eye could see. Children walked or sat in dazed conditions waiting to die, their stomachs distended, eyes bulging, the flesh on their faces no further from the bone than their skin. They died by the thousands from lack of food or care, or from contamination and the growing red festering spots that blistered, pussed, and scarred.

Weeks passed and Zaynab's child now weighed only five pounds. His legs were withered appendages to a round, pock-marked body, joined to a head without hair. Zaynab's breasts sagged in useless defeat as she lay down beside him, weakly waving her hand in a vain effort to keep flies away from his eyes and lips. "Oh, God in heaven, Allah be praised. I lie down and rest, alhamdulillah." The mother and child finally found their peace, drifting into a semi-coma, then to their eternal sleep.

Was this natural disaster inevitable and an evil trick of Mother Nature, or an accident that could have been avoided? Had Allah permitted this devastation, or had it been caused by man? Could the depth of the water flow that year have been known in advance and the speed of the impending flood predicted or prevented?

> *"My greatest strength is the love for my people.*
> *My greatest weakness is that I love them too much."*
> *–Sheikh Mujibur Rahman*

In ancient times some people used celestial observation to predict the future. They would look to the sun, moon, and stars for answers. The forecaster knew after the setting of the next sun that the new moon would appear, and the gods would tell him the future, if the people would live or die. When the sliver of the new moon tilted like a bowl with both horns level, so no water could fall out, it was a sign of impending drought.

At sunset the forecaster gathered his ceremonial garb about him. Operating under the authority of the primitive tribal chief, he muttered incantations and threw dust into the wind. The tribal elders had assembled to watch and wait to see what the forecaster would predict. The sun fell down and heavy night crept across the sky. A thick mist obscured the villagers' direct view, but in the distance a single drumbeat was heard, followed by another. The telegram that sounded from observation hill was one beat, then two, followed by three and one.

A wild cheer wailed up in the crowd and exploded. With one voice the shouts shot up and bounced off the sky as local drums of celebration began to beat in elaborate synchronized sequence. The gods had given life! The new moon was tilted so water could flow from heaven. Food would grow and life would be restored. The singing, dancing, and lovemaking began with vigor, and gyrations continued to exhaustion long into the night.

One might be tempted to look back across eons of time and laugh at the ignorant savage ancestors who worshiped the moon. They're all gone now, but wonder remains. Were these really simple savages, who believed blindly in the weather mythologies and futures foretold by the forecaster, or did they all just anticipate needing some great excuse for throwing a wild party?

Generations passed.

An enlightened man in his biplane was flying high above the clouds of New Mexico. He slowed his craft and heaved out a heavy block of dry ice into the very center of the largest cloud over his farm.

Landing back at his fields he secured the plane and walked across to his barn in his own private celebration to await the inevitable deluge of rain that would now certainly come. All he found, however, was a large hole smashed through his roof where he'd thrown out the ice block. The only wonder is why he never told anyone.

Possibly, ancient celebrations were not only a lot more fun, but far more productive and rational than modern ones.

******

In 1930 August Veraart of Holland was obsessed with discovering the cause of precipitation. His Fokker biplane was in the air at first light. The pilot in the front open-air seat guided the plane over the North Sea Canal toward the west coast. From the rear seat Veraart continually scanned the skies to the West and South. If the winds were proper, the afternoon heat would rise cumulus clouds.

Veraart cupped his hands and yelled forward above the engine noise, pointing northeast as they flew over the coastal breakwaters. By midmorning the rising condensation of fog could be seen accumulating in exactly the hoped-for patterns.

"This looks like the day. Take her back."

The pilot banked right 180 degrees to return to the field. Flaring out, the plane settled on the forward landing gear and slowed as the tail skid dragged along the turf. Within two hours the hand-operated grinder was affixed to the rear compartment floor and the pair were off again, this time heading north by northwest, rising above the clouds in high anticipation.

This was indeed the day, the first in history.

Above the large central group of clouds, the pilot slowed the craft. "Maintain the attitude straight southwest. Keep it just above a stall." Veraart began to madly crank away on the dry ice grinder that spewed particles through the clouds below.

Back on the ground smiles grew into handshakes, hugs, and cheers as it began to rain. It rained on all their upturned faces. It rained on their shoes. It rained on their matted down hair, drizzled down their cheeks, and dripped off their noses, all to the sounds of celebration. The first manmade rain in history was above their heads and falling at their feet.

From there the celebrations escalated quickly.

Along with Veraart's early experiments, famed meteorologists Tor Bergeron in Sweden and Walter Findeisen in Germany had also been working hard to observe and document causes of precipitation. Bergeron is credited for having first advanced the concepts that clouds contain both super-cooled water and ice crystals, that natural rain is the result of very rapid growth in the size of water droplets in clouds, and that water droplets are coincident with the formation of ice crystals within the cloud formations. Bergeron further reasoned that ice crystals are natural nuclei around which snow or rain drops form and depending on the temperature below the clouds, how we get either snow or rain.

The 1930s were not great years in Germany for independent scientists. Nazi forces were rapidly gathering. Yet, working within that difficult environment, Walter Findeisen's endorsements and refinement of Bergeron's theories are what helped establish today's generally accepted science of precipitation formation and cloud physics. The process involved for ice crystal growth that occurs in mixed phase clouds would later become widely known within the scientific community as the Bergeron-Findeisen process.

Walter Findeisen's work had helped progress weather science to the next logical step, that of actively demonstrating how artificial nuclei could be introduced into clouds on a calculated basis by man. Further tests and trials in cloud physics held true. Dry ice dissipation, or the artificial "cold-rain" process worked!

More scientific "cloud-breaking" breakthroughs would come forth around 1946 with the discovery of dependable methods for silver iodide generation by Vincent Schaefer, his colleague Dr. Bernard Vonnegut, and many others, but not quite yet. Weather researchers were rapidly advancing how to coax untapped moisture potential from the clouds, but politics would first try to dominate and control the world from them.

*"Only as you gasp your dying breath shall you
understand, your life amounted to no more than
one drop in a limitless ocean.
Yet what is any ocean, but a multitude of drops?"*

–David Mitchell, Cloud Atlas

Prague, 1940

The usual photograph of Adolph Hitler hung over his writing table in the office of the Assistant Deputy Minister of Science.

"Herr Professor Doctor Findeisen," said the uniformed man sitting across his desk, "Of course, Germany requires your full cooperation."

Dr. Walter Findeisen looked past the man seeking some kind of recognition or cue from his colleague, the Assistant Deputy Minister. An immediate flash of realization appeared in his mind, a nightmare vision of his laboratory being turned into some minor machine cog for the growing war effort. Only for that particular moment, and never again, would Findeisen see himself as only a minor cog in the war machine.

It would've been impossible for anyone to have missed seeing the line of black cars that arrived that morning, especially the one carrying a Major who wore the Death's Head symbol on his cap and double lightning bolts on his lapels. That SS Major now sat casually here in their office. The armed sergeant, Feldwebel Hofmann, stood just outside the door to the right with Korporal Schmidt on the left. What could he do but cooperate, or at least appear to cooperate?

The Assistant Deputy Minister of Science felt sweat running down the back of his shirt collar. "Herr Doctor, Major Kieger is here today to instruct you in your new duties." The Major nodded. Then, as previously arranged, the Assistant Deputy left the room, leaving the two alone with the armed guards posted outside the door.

"But of course. What can I do to be of service?"

"Herr Doctor Findeisen, obviously I would not be here without having first conducted an exhaustive background inquiry of your record. The work you have been conducting is most interesting and has come to the attention of the Reichsleitung. I am here under the authority of Dr. Heinrich Himmler. Everything I say from this point on must be protected under the highest security. Disclosure of confidential information without written authority carries with it the most severe penalties. Do you understand, Herr Doctor?"

"I understand, Herr Major."

"Before I go on I must insist you execute your signature upon certain documents."

The Major took some papers from an attaché case and placed them upon the desk. They bore several official stamps and seals acknowledging receipt of confidential information. Dr. Findeisen looked through the papers quickly. The final page contained concise wording of a personal oath of fealty and allegiance to the Feuhrer, Adolph Hitler.

Findeisen had heard of these kinds of oaths but seeing such a document in his name bearing the official stamps of the Reich Chancellor's office startled him, causing him to hesitate and go pale. He felt himself get faint, the blood quickly draining from his face.

"Is there anything wrong, Herr Doctor?" questioned the Major, his right hand resting on the black leather holster holding the nine-millimeter P-38 automatic pistol belted at his side.

Findeisen quickly composed himself. "No, I don't think so," he said hurriedly. "I just need a pen."

The Major produced a thick fountain pen from the attaché case and laid it on the desk in front of him. It didn't take long.

"Doctor, we have three principal matters of immediate interest with you. The first, as you know, is that accurate artillery trajectory calculations are dependent to a degree on knowledge of upper air temperature gradients and velocities. Certain guns now being designed are of such a nature that temperature gradient calculations are of the utmost importance. Second, rocket propulsion technology has given the Reich a new tool for strengthening our field operations. Pilotless rocket propelled missiles will have the capability of outreaching even our largest guns. Again, temperature and air gradients will significantly affect the performance of these missiles. Third, it's been noted you have been able to produce recently some measurable results in weather modification. Doctor, certainly I need not describe to you the importance of improving such advances. Our most sophisticated systems operations and control centers must have accurate weather reports. Then imagine the advantages we will have through the ability not only to predict the weather, but to fine tailor it to our advantage. Der Feuhrer has expressed a personal interest in this matter."

Dr. Findeisen made a last, futile attempt to minimize his own importance in all of this. "Yes, but what can I do? This is purely speculative science."

"Tomorrow morning your personal escorts will arrive to take you to Reichswetterdienst. You will be given priority coordination authority along with requisition authority related to the projects I have mentioned. Aircraft will be made available as you may need them to further your experiments. I personally congratulate you."

"Thank you. I don't quite know what to say."

"Say nothing, Herr Doctor. Feldwebel Hofmann will accompany you until your staff officers arrive tomorrow. Now, if you will excuse me, I have some pressing personal plans for this evening." Major Krieger collected the signed papers and turned toward the door, "Heil Hitler!" The click of his heels and strike of his boots on the hardwood floor echoed through the room long after he had gone.

Findeisen was not a prophet and did not see himself as a forecaster. He knew he could not predict the future, but he had a pretty good idea of the near term consequences if he did not accept what was about to be required of him. Historians would later speculate that Findeisen intentionally withheld information from his subsequent reports, but Findeisen clearly understood if Major Krieger had any such speculation there would have been no future for him.

Findeisen discovered later that Feldwebel Hofmann was actually Hans Hofmann, a lettered university student in physics and astronomy who actively contributed to his continued research. It was only a few years later when Findeisen and Hofmann, along with other of their colleagues, were captured by the Soviet Union with all their research records.

Hofmann went on to work toward the development of new weather modification theories in the Soviet Union. While their personal worlds changed dramatically several times during these formative, early years, what they accomplished and pioneered together changed the entire world forever.

******

Numerous weather modification experiments were conducted by the Soviet Union during the 1940s and '50s through the Central Aerological Observatory, the Institute of Geophysics of the Georgian Academy of Sciences, and the Leningrad Institute of Experimental Meteorology, which became part of the Voeikov Main Geophysical Observatory, or MGO. MGO is the original meteorological institution of Russia, still focused today on weather control, climate modeling, applied climatology, cloud physics, and hydrodynamic, long-term weather forecasting.

By the mid-1960s the Soviets were expending millions of dollars a year on resources, as was the United States, for active weather modification projects. In the United States the federal agencies which were participating in publicly known weather modification research included the Departments of Agriculture, Interior, Commerce, Army, Navy, Air Force, NASA, and the National Science Foundation.

Of some noteworthy significance, the United States covertly conducted Operation Popeye during the Vietnam War, using cloud seeding over the Ho Chi Minh trail system to dramatically increase rainfall there, hoping to create enough year-round moisture to keep the trails impassable with mud to reduce troop movements and infiltration. The top-secret operation ran from 1967–1972, with sorties carried out from Thailand by the 54th Weather Reconnaissance Squadron under the code name "Motorpool."

The Soviet Union, however, excelled and exemplified its commitment to weather modification experiments and production operations by a five-to-one margin over the United States. Wealthy farmers from both countries were also enamored by many innovative civilian entrepreneurs claiming to be able to bring more rain to their parched land, or to artificially suppress crop-damaging hail storms. The race for global weather dominance was on!

> *"Behind the scenes, while statesmen argue policies and engineers build space satellites, other men are working day and night. They are quiet men, so little known to the public that the magnitude of their job, when you first hear of it, staggers the imagination. Their object is to control the weather and change the face of the world. Some of these men are Americans. Others are Russians. The first skirmishes of an undeclared cold war between them already have been fought. Unless a peace is achieved the war's end will determine whether Russia or the United States rules the earth's thermometers."*
>
> *–Frances Leighton, May 25, 1958,*
> *in The American Weekly*

Washington D.C., September 1968

The office of the Secretary of Defense is the inner circle of the Pentagon. "George, this is critically important. I've got to have absolute confidence that consistent information comes up here to the top. I want you to personally head up the implementation stages for Blue Condor."

The Secretary of Defense kept pacing back and forth as he continued. "You'll be working with staff officers appointed directly under authority of the Joint Chiefs. You will have the title of Under Secretary of Defense. You will report solely to me and no one else. We can't continue to permit the old games of interagency politics and departmental budget-grab horse shit. Seriously, if the services get themselves all locked up fighting over this operation and start playing games about who is in charge we could actually end up with the whole damn world out of kilter."

"Okay, so what's Blue Condor?" At that point George Radkin had never heard of Blue Condor and he'd just been appointed to be Under Secretary of Defense for guiding its implementation, whatever that meant.

George looked perplexed. "Don't worry about it, George, it's just an operations code name. This one has more potential than any other I've ever been involved with, though. It's going to drive significant new environmental research. We just formed it and it's going to bring together a lot of important cutting-edge work from the services and many other agencies, trust me. First thing tomorrow I'd like you back in Monmouth for a briefing by General West. He's my top security man there. I think I've got another good security man committed specifically for this operation, too."

George felt slightly more comfortable hearing his new assignment was related to environmental research. He was not a military man. He was a civilian by nature and disposition. George Radkin was happily married and had three children, two girls and a young boy. He'd graduated from the University of Oklahoma in mathematics and chemistry, taking a doctorate in physics from Cal Tech in 1948, no small feat for an Oklahoma farm boy. He'd been working on Army research and development in communications at Fort Monmouth, New Jersey for the past twenty-two years. He had never met this General West, though, not even heard of him.

It took George a little over three hours to drive back from the Pentagon parking garage home to Red Bank. He didn't mind the occasional drive down the turnpike into D.C., the only problem was he couldn't ever tell his wife anything he talked about while there. Some of the guys thought that was a benefit.

George arrived the next morning and checked the location twice. The building didn't have a number or a name. It was just there. It wasn't really at Fort Monmouth. It was maybe six miles or so south of Red Bank and sported the usual array of communications microwave antenna and fencing.

The building was six floors of concrete secured by private guards. It was one of those places of undisclosed location, where the fact it existed at all was classified as secret. He stepped inside the outer door and presented his ID at the desk. When the desk agent realized who he was, he stood up and saluted him awkwardly. He then pressed a button under the desk and the steel-reinforced inner door buzzed open.

General West was there inside to meet him. He stepped out from a side room, shook George's hand firmly and led him down the hall into George's new corner office, where he handed over to him all the personnel files for everyone on his team, including prospects.

It looked like this was going to be a nice place to work, with a beautiful mahogany desk, bookshelves, and rich flooring. For being an executive corner office, though, it didn't have any windows, so there wasn't any kind of view.

One by one he and the General went through the files together. George's first major team meeting was scheduled in two weeks, but after moving into the position of Under Secretary of Defense and getting settled, it took him almost a full year to pull everything together for presenting the initial test project.

******

Victor Sine's personnel file was impressive. It showed that after he left the Army he had worked as a legal prosecutor in Queens County, New York. After three years there he left prosecution to become a Special Agent for the FBI. From the FBI he went to the CIA, and presently he'd been working as a special operations officer for the CIA in domestic affairs.

The record said Sine had developed informants in the Mafia, worked in Kansas City and Chicago, and tracked two subversives through New York, Pittsburgh, and over to Kent State in Ohio. The Secretary of Defense had recommended him as a Chief of Security and everything appeared to be in order. He certainly seemed more than qualified to be selected as a top national security man.

Sine's earliest military assignment was in West Germany where he spent two years with the NATO liaison officer for international affairs at Supreme Headquarters Allied Powers Europe (SHAPE) in Brussels, Belgium. He had traveled for several years after this between Brussels, the command offices at Heidelberg (CENTAG – the Central Army Group), and the British Army of the Rhein (NORTHAG Headquarters – the Northern Army Group) near Koln.

What the personnel record did not show was that Victor Sine prided himself on extreme self-mastery. Fear of any kind, or of any person or situation, was to him considered a weakness which must be conquered at any price. He liked to collect artifacts which he viewed as symbols of strength. It was in Germany when he'd began his personal collection of war souvenirs. He never forgot the time he found one particularly special prize.

He was walking west along a small street in Heidelberg from the Rathouse and town square. There were several small antique stores lining the street. He was taking his time that day, enjoying casual window shopping and people watching when one antique shop in particular caught his attention. There was a large brass double-panned scale displayed in the window, the type used as a symbol of justice, except this one was huge. The pans were hammered copper and almost a full meter in diameter. The cross-bar and chains were made of carefully pounded steel, "probably by some grizzled old blacksmith," Sine thought. As he walked over to the window to get a closer look, that was when he saw the special prize. There it was, lying unceremoniously beneath the scale, partially hidden by the window sill, right next to its matching-black, unstrapped leather case and belt.

He turned into the shop instantly, trying hard not to look too interested in buying anything in particular. He glanced around the small shop nonchalantly, paused a few seconds to examine some insignificant items, and then finally moved over by the large scale in the window.

"Wie viele mark kosten dis 9mm parabellum?" His German wasn't great, but it was enough to get by.

The store owner came over and answered in flawless English, "425 marks, including the holster and belt. It's in almost perfect condition, common serial numbers on all parts. A Walther P-38 in such condition is rare. This one is certainly a treasure."

The circled swastika clasped in claws of an eagle with outspread wings was debossed in the leather and stamped into the metal. When he picked it up a voice from history's ghost tingled through his fingers and whispered in his ear. He paid full price immediately and never forgot the feeling, or the sound.

George Radkin called the meeting to order at precisely 10:30 on the Monday morning of September 29, 1969. It was in the conference room of the third floor of The Bunker. At least that's what the staff had been calling it, and the name stuck. It wasn't because the building was supposed to have a name. It wasn't. It just needed to be called something other than, "that six story concrete building south of Red Bank, New Jersey."

The conference room was interesting, but not obvious. It was located in the center of the building and was really two rooms, one inside the other. There was a two-meter gap of blank space between the rooms, all the way around, on all four sides and top and bottom.

The inner room was resting on sensitive insolation cushions with a maze of electronic interception and jamming gear meshed around the inner space. Electric power was passed into the room through special filters and the ventilation system was insulated and completely self-contained. The design engineer said only a Harvard graduate cockroach could bug that room.

The room was decorated in masculine deep greens and browns with a large walnut table in the center, circled by twenty-five soft-green high-back chairs, ten of which were occupied this morning. There was nothing there to tell the time of day except for the beautifully large ceramic and wood electric pendulum clock hung by George on the east wall. The clock was a gift. There had been a party held for George when he left the Pentagon and a friend had collected money from other employees. Of course, the design engineer didn't know anything about the clock or how it had gotten there.

"There is a packet of material on the table at each of your chairs. Inside is a synopsis of each report with a blank note pad and pencil." Victor Sine held up one of the packets as he spoke to the group. "To assist your memory you may take notes with the pencils provided. All material, including the notes, must remain visible on the table at all times. You will not be permitted to take anything from this room, neither during break or at the end of the meeting."

Sine went on to complete the rest of his usual security briefing, then George Radkin stood and began his rehearsed remarks.

"Gentlemen," said George, for there were no women present, "Our internal staff review for each of the separate service projects indicates that we should move next to live site testing. The final bench tests are completed now, all with positive results. Our first live implementation shall be known henceforth as 'Falcon Flyer'. Several possible locations were considered. Your packets contain summary evaluations of all the possible sites, but with emphasis on the final two, which my team has submitted for your consideration and determination today. The principal criteria used to make our final selections was the ability to easily measure results under optimally-controlled conditions."

Clearing his throat, George continued, "There are just two places on the globe which are most conducive to all the testing requirements." He then reached forward and began to unfold a large, laminated map that was at the center of the table.

Everyone around the table was eerily quiet as George spread out the map. The big electric clock on the wall could be heard humming in the background.

"First, and primarily, we need a location with

exceptionally unstable weather conditions. The test results must be able to be measured accurately and communicated back to us effectively and of course with complete secrecy. Any budget considerations for continuing this project further will depend upon a successful, live, site test."

Several of the men in the room opened their packets and started thumbing through the reports, listening more intently now.

"You will note the two most acceptable sites are along the windward northern areas of the Hawaiian Islands and the coastal areas north of the Bay of Bengal. Some of the heaviest rainfalls in the world occur at these locations."

"Wait a minute!"

"Yes, General West?"

"Of all the possible locations you've reviewed, your team is seriously suggesting we take this project to our own shores first?"

Slightly put-off, but not surprised at all by the General's interruption, George Radkin responded to him carefully. "The long-term importance of this project requires us to consider all of the best sites which exemplify optimal conditions for the post-test evaluation," said George calmly. "This is why we are here today, gentlemen. However, we are only selecting the initial test site at this time. Full implementation of Blue Condor is ten years away, at least, and that's only if full implementation is ever granted. There are many more decisions to be made before then. What we do now is present our best test site recommendations for your consideration. I do not have any approval authority to proceed further without your unanimous consent and advice."

George paused for emphasis, then continued after sitting

back down, "Regardless of which test site you choose today, the ultimate effect of this decision is to bring about a dramatic change in the weather for our own shores. Actually, if proven successful, this test should affect most of the northern hemispheric weather systems, including not only the weather in Hawaii, but also across the continental states from California to New York."

Everyone in the room was now looking at George. He scanned quickly around the table. "Admiral Wainsmith, do you have a question?"

"Yes, of course. My primary concern with choosing to test in the Pacific is the safety of our fleet and support facilities there. The Navy must also consider operational security and budget. If any equipment or reporting facilities did happen to become damaged as a result of the Falcon Flyer test, it would be difficult for the Navy to conceal this project from any inquiry that might come from Congressional sources."

The Admiral stood and held up his packet to the group, making reference to the various reports of shipboard and Marine readiness data received by air flight courier the night before and added only that morning. He then stated what should've already been obvious. "Only the ten of us here in this room are really aware of the importance for ensuring a successful and untraceable test. So far security has been optimal, but we can never know for sure about leaks. We need to be very, very careful."

Victor Sine scowled and muttered silently to himself, "So far you say? Worried about leaks? My security is perfect. There are not going to be any leaks unless it's from your fat ass."

Admiral Wainsmith lowered himself back down into his chair confidently. "I doubt even the Secretary of Defense or the

Joint Chiefs fully realize the significance and far-reaching implications of this operation," said the Admiral slowly. "We have all been careful to control reported budget expenditures and protect against auditing, but I must say that I agree with General West. We shouldn't hold this first test on our own shores." The Admiral grimaced. "We can't risk testing in the Pacific right now, the timing and optics are bad. Plus, if we do end up bringing down significant damage to any of our Navy facilities in Hawaii this is going to mean new budget scrutiny and probably an additional delay for our planned base expansion and development on the leeward side of Oahu. George, can you please give us a summary description of your second site?"

George stood again and extended a pointer to indicate the sea east of India, tapping on the map at the center of the table. "The Bay of Bengal, located here, lies between the equator and the Tropic of Cancer. The prevailing equatorial air currents naturally pump warm, moist air from the southwest in the summer. The upper air currents reverse in the winter to bring in colder elements from the northeast. We believe the southeast monsoon and shifting winds from the northeast in the late fall and early winter seasons will provide us the most unstable air masses to work with. These air masses can then be followed easily by radar and direct observation from both land and sea. Our own teams' local observation requirements could be supported by the 7th fleet, which is already operating in the Indian Ocean."

Glancing over at Admiral Wainsmith, hoping for a nod or some other indication of his tacit approval, George Radkin continued. "For interagency reports the necessary cover for our teams' presence there can be attributed to increasing Middle East tensions, which requires movement of our fleet and air support. The north of the Bay of Bengal is East Pakistan, inhabited by the Bengali people who are primarily Muslim. It's likely that the Hindu leaders in India can be expected to support troop movements of any of our military forces within the area, so we should be able to remain almost entirely insulated from attracting too much political scrutiny."

"The necessary cyclonic effect should be relatively straightforward to trigger anywhere in this area," George said, tapping his pointer against the map again. "Most importantly, once triggered it should be simple for us to demonstrate how the increased rain, wind strength, and directional enhancements were accomplished precisely through the direct application of this technology. Proving out our success factors should be obvious."

He then paused, taking a few seconds to look directly into the eyes of each man seated around the room. "Even if these rain conditions set new world records, and the airflow patterns from the resultant cyclone are observed and studied extensively by civilian stations, which we fully expect, we do not expect any substantial questioning will come from the population about unnatural causes, no matter how the effects play out. The local governments in that region lack the ability to understand or deal with sophisticated scientific procedures. In fact, the primary government in West Pakistan may not even realize what's happened or respond at all."

"Following the test," said George, "we will fly in our post-evaluation teams under the guise of civilian relief support for the area. Our teams can arrive together with the expected humanitarian responders and non-profit groups who will be bringing in standard first aid, medical supplies, and foodstuff materials. That sort of response and call for volunteers happens routinely after every major storm in this area of the world."

George sat back down again, satisfied at his presentation, and returned the map pointer to his jacket pocket. "In summation," he said self-assuredly, "we believe the Falcon Flyer test should be able to proceed well there without detection and at minimum budget requirement. Evacuation plans were established by the Pakistani government several years ago and any extensive damage should be limited primarily to property loss only. The entire test sequence should take less than three days. After that we'll be able to start compiling the results."

There was an awkward silence in the room as each man tried to process what they'd just heard, wondering whether or not to ask any further questions, then finally Victor Sine stood up. "Gentlemen, I suggest at this point we allow the next hour for each of you to discuss this recommendation amongst yourselves and individually review the packet material," gesturing to George's envelope laying on the table next to him. "We will then take a ten-minute break and reconvene this meeting for your decision."

Radkin and Sine retired to the administrative offices north of the conference room. Vic congratulated George on his presentation and both laughed together about seeing Admiral Wainsmith's face when he'd realized Hawaii was in final consideration as the test site.

"I was told he has a vacation home in Kapolei, but I didn't know that old bastard had such a significant new Navy property interest in Oahu."

They both had anticipated the Admiral's response to the Hawaii suggestion. "Maybe his base expansion is still only in the planning stages. In any event, the reports are pretty clear either site will do, and the packets are well arranged."

When the meeting reconvened the predictable result and decision was made. Falcon Flyer would land in one year on the shoulder of the Bay of Bengal. East Pakistan was perfect, and besides, who the hell cared about Bangladesh anyway?

Kiev, 1968

"We can actually place the device anywhere. There is no transmitter. It's just a hollow resonating box set to our precise dimensions and material specifications. No power is required. It responds to voice frequencies."

"How can something like that operate?"

"When the box is in place, the small hole on this side is open to the room to be monitored. The box can be placed into a wall during construction, made a part of furniture like a desk or table, or placed into nearly anything."

"Ya, you said that already, but how does it work? I don't understand."

"Well, maybe it's better if we demonstrate."

The lower level of the laboratory building in Kiev had three main rooms in a row down one long hall. A low frequency microwave transmitter had been set up in the south room. A broad band high efficiency dish antenna connected to an exceptionally sensitive receiver was installed in the north.

"Herr Comrade Hofmann, please place the box at the center of the table."

Hans Hofmann had been working at the Kiev laboratory for the past three years. His degrees in physics and astronomy, along with his association with Dr. Findeisen, had given him unique qualifications. After being captured by the Russians, he'd found himself assigned to the laboratory, tasked with running experimentations on a combination of electronic communication, weather modification, and nuclear physics. He'd been there now more than twenty years. Most recently he'd been assigned to experiments related to intelligence gathering techniques using microwave frequencies.

Initially after his capture Hoffman's mind had dwelt on possible escape, but years had faded those thoughts into the distance. He had honestly become comfortable with his assigned enticements for working in the new laboratory and the lower direct oversight there. He was told where to work and when he could come and go, but freedom to do anything at pleasure after hours was never an issue here. Hofmann did as he was told, the same as in the SS. His routines hadn't changed all that much, his commander just wore a different uniform. Life was habit.

He placed the box down as instructed, and a tape player was turned on. The sound of a Soviet radio announcer suddenly filled the room and the small box at the center of the table. In the south room the low frequency microwave transmitter was turned on and its antenna pointed through the center room where they were all gathered, toward the direction of the north room at the opposite side.

"It's really quite a simple concept. The box resonates to voice sound frequencies. Microwaves are directed to penetrate through the room and are slightly modulated or changed when part of them pass through the box. At the other end we just run the computer program to remove all of the original microwave signal and what remains is the part changed by the transmission through the box. We can pick up a whisper. In fact, we can distinguish one whisper from another. Each person's voice has a certain characteristic imprint. The computer can even be programmed so it's able to eliminate everything except a specific requested voice print pattern. This way we can remove any background noise or interference from sound jamming devices."

"What kind of range?"

"We have tested the device over a 500-meter distance through a concrete building. We simply place the transmitter on one side and the receiver on the other. There is no way of detecting the box or finding where it is located. The components give off absolutely no transmission. It's just a box and could be anywhere."

Hofmann and his associate kept talking as they walked with the small group out into the hallway, leaving the tape recording of the radio announcer playing alone in the center room. "There are actually three parts to the system: the box, the modulator, and a memory module. The modulator is electronic, about the size of a deck of cards, and it's entirely self-contained. The location of the modulator must be precisely calculated in its proximity to the resonating box. The circuits in the memory module collect and store digital codes representing the intercepted sound waves. The codes are then retained in microchip memory until retrieved."

"Okay, but how do you get the information out?"

"The easiest way is to have the system built into an electronic host device with a 110-volt, sixty-cycle power supply. That specification is most common among the Americans. When the device is plugged into a power outlet, we can then hear everything in the room where the device is located. It's best if we can get access to the main circuit box and are able to transmit along through the power lines. Unfortunately, listening devices that transmit data using fluctuations sent through power lines is a commonly known surveillance technique and its effectiveness can be all too easily eliminated simply by adding filters to the lines."

"However, there is another retrieval method we've discovered and successfully tested. Low frequency microwaves scatter across a broad area, but higher frequencies can be specifically directed, like a pointer, and encoded with programming. This means that after the device is in place, we can direct a specially encoded high frequency microwave transmission through the box to turn on the modulator and collect the data. The modulator modifies the microwaves as the data is sent. The receiver on the other side interprets the changes, eliminating the original coded signal so only the collected sound recording remains. This method allows us an additional data collection opportunity in cases where direct access to the power circuits is not possible."

"Ahh, yes, that's very interesting. So, into what types of devices have you tried installing the components thus far?"

"We can install the components into really anything that normally plugs into a power source. There is a slight hum from the modulator whenever it's turned on and operating, but it's fairly negligible. The hum can be masked by other sounds. We've tested the device effectively using an electric clock that has a second hand that also hums."

"This is good news, Comrade! Our source in Washington says something big is being planned and there's soon to be a newly appointed Under Secretary of Defense to direct a new clandestine operation. Their suggestion is we give the new appointee a clock as a gift. If it's elaborate and beautiful enough hopefully he will display it prominently somewhere of significance and then forget about it, like on his personal office wall."

"Presenting the clock as a gift? Won't that be too

obvious?"

"Not necessarily. Our agent suggested using a cover story of collecting a few dollars from his friends around the office. Arrangements can be made to suggest a local merchant of our choosing. There will no doubt be a celebration party. It will appear like the gift came to him from a few close and trusted friends, nothing suspicious."

"What kind of lead time is needed to make this happen?"

"Our diplomatic courier can have all components in Washington tomorrow if needed."

> *"If an unfriendly nation solves the problem of*
> *weather control and gets into the position to*
> *control the large-scale weather patterns before we*
> *can, the results could be even more disastrous than*
> *nuclear warfare."*
>
> *–Captain Howard T. Orville, Chairman of the*
> *President's Advisory Committee on Weather Control,*
> *January 1, 1958, in the Pasadena Star- News*

Early in November of 1970, the United States Navy 7th Fleet was dispatched to the Indian Ocean. The fleet was requested to help establish a strong and visible military presence there in the wake of increasing political tensions in the Middle East. There were also several government scientists sent out unremarkably along with the fleet to monitor the various unstable weather patterns within the region.

Military aircraft had been used for years to fly into hurricanes for wind measurement and storm monitoring purposes. It didn't seem unusual that weather watchers were interested in the cyclone, which had developed there in the Bay of Bengal.

On November 12, 1970, an immense flood hit East Pakistan. Rainfall swelled all the rivers. The deluge surged toward the sea only to be met by a huge wall of water rising back to meet it with the incoming tide, heaving far inland because of the cyclone out in the Bay of Bengal. Hundreds of miles were buried as the flood waters washed and flowed back and forth from hill to sea until the earth was littered with bodies and debris.

The world watched disinterestedly as Falcon Flyer flapped its wings all around the Bay of Bengal. Very few knew the damn bird even existed. The whole world simply thought this storm was yet another sick-and-twisted act of God. The test, however, had been an undisputed success. The storm generation had been clearly visible by satellite and on radar.

This area of the world was accustomed to natural disasters. Back in October of 1737, a terrible cyclone had whipped the Indian Ocean into a fury and moved through the Bay of Bengal with a vengeance, lifting the sea by more than twenty feet and drowning 300,000 people. Almost the same thing happened again in November of 1970. The difference was way back in 1737 no one could have predicted its coming. In 1970 there were several people who knew, just not the people who died there.

As a result of prior storm disasters, the Pakistani government had developed extensive evacuation plans for the region during the 1960s. The plans had been rehearsed and practiced, yet when this disaster came no evacuation order was given. There were no runners sent to sound the alarm. As the intense severity of this storm had been almost entirely unexpected, the death-filled waters simply carried their own message.

Following usual protocols, world-wide relief services were sent in after the storm to try to help the distressed. Small scientific teams were moved in along with the relief services, assessing and quietly reporting back details about the storm's effects, as gruesome starvation and disease set in among the newly homeless thousands.

Back at The Bunker encrypted messages began to arrive, with the daily decoding key turning jumbled sentences back into recognizable written intelligence reports. Victor Sine was elated more and more with each passing day because of the incoming news about the mission's success. On Thursday he spontaneously decided to take his secretary away with him to Atlantic City for an extended weekend. Sine strutted around the offices, seeming like an omniscient God, except for the tasteless dirty jokes he was telling as he and his much younger employee left early that afternoon.

George felt a rising disgust when Vic's wife called the next morning and he overheard the operator saying Mr. Sine had been sent on a special assignment for the weekend. "No, I really can't tell you more. You must understand our security requirements. The nature of the assignment is classified information."

George Radkin was experiencing severely mixed emotions. It wasn't entirely Vic's personal behavior that disturbed him. It was the test. Certainly, by any measure, the Falcon Flyer test had been deemed a resounding success by everyone involved, but he hadn't anticipated the extent of the devastation. The dark images sent in the photos received with the reports were dead people. Why hadn't the Pakistani government given the expected warning? George called his wife and said he wouldn't be home that night. He stayed at The Bunker.

The ultimate weapon had just been tested, *and* it had worked beyond anything yet imagined! George reached into the bottom drawer of his desk and opened a bottle of scotch that was stashed there. He remembered back to an earlier conversation he'd had with Sine in June, five months earlier.

"George, do you realize what we've got here? People have been talking about building the ultimate weapon for generations, but they've missed the point."

"What do you mean?"

"Everyone always talks about bullets or bombs or laser guns, whatever makes the biggest boom. Military forces have always had what's referred to as unidentifiable devices, devices that can't be traced to any particular country of manufacture. Well, take that idea to the next level. Imagine, George, a weapon that wipes out the enemy completely, but everyone thinks it was simply an act of God or a quirk of nature."

"An untraceable weapon."

"Exactly! It's like having the power to go out and rape any woman you like, any time you choose, but not only does she not realize she was intentionally raped, she reasons it's a test from God. Maybe she even has a spiritual experience as a result. This boggles my mind, George, yet we've got it. We've got it!"

George wondered silently if Sine had completely lost all sense of decency. He wondered if he had also lost his. He'd specifically been given the title Under Secretary of Defense, so he could carry out this ongoing operation without fear that any military commanders who needed to be involved would hesitate or refuse cooperation.

As he sat and drank George heard a tiny whispered voice in his ear, "It's okay because you're in charge. Just think about how bad things might be if Vic Sine were in charge." George looked around the room, half expecting to find someone else there in his office with him. "You're really a hero here," continued the reassuring whispering voice. "Relax, everything's going to be okay because you can control this."

He was then struck with a chastening sense of realization that the voice was coming only from himself. Pandora's box was wide open, and he knew now it would never be shut. He took another long drink from the bottle and envisioned holding the smiling Gorgon's head in his clenched fist as blood dripped down from its severed neck.

George Radkin shuddered at the thought of staring straight into the face that had brought so much sorrow and death. He started to weep uncontrollably. He didn't know Zaynab bint-Ahmad's name, but in his mind's eye he could clearly see her emaciated face, and that of her child, and that of all the other innumerable thousands dead.

Victor Sine saw only unlimited power.

"Unlimited power is the ideal thing when it is in safe hands. The despotism of heaven is the one absolutely perfect government, and earthly despotism would be the absolute perfect earthly government if the conditions were the same; namely the despot the perfectest individual of the human race, and his lease of life perpetual; but as a perishable, perfect man must die and leave his despotism in the hands of an imperfect successor, an earthly despotism is not merely a bad form of government, it is the worst form that is possible."

–Mark Twain

Three years after the cyclone had devastated East Pakistan, John Wayment and Scott Watson graduated with honors from UCLA. Lifelong friends, the two parted ways soon thereafter.

John worked while in school as the weekend weather forecaster at his local television station, and just prior to graduation, had been sending out resumes madly to various regional and national television stations. He'd included video clips of his best broadcasts and followed up with letters and personal phone calls. His first choice was San Francisco, but he was still excited to receive a call one evening from the office of the General Manager of KWGN-TV in Denver, Colorado.

He was on the airplane for Denver that next Monday morning, leaving LAX International at 6:00 AM, to arrive in time for his ten o'clock appointment. John told Sharon he hoped to be back that evening, otherwise he would call.

John had met Sharon in his third year at UCLA. He was finishing up a history class series and she had sat down in the seat next to him on the front row on the very first day. He'd noticed her very attractive knees first, before working up the courage to look her in the eyes.

"I guess I'm a knee man," he had thought. Now they had been married for fifteen months and Sharon was expecting their first child in September.

"Take care of little what's its name," he had said as he patted her on the stomach before climbing into the cab for the airport. "I should be back tonight." John had kissed her. It wasn't a long and passionate kiss. After all, he was only going to Denver for the day.

Sharon had responded with a smile, "Just remember it's your little what's its name in here. Be careful and come home to me."

When he did come home that evening Sharon was there waiting to pick him up at the airport. "How did it go?"

"Good, how's the little one been?"

"Fine. Everything is totally fine here. So, what happened there?"

"Oh, nothing much," he had said, squirming and trying unsuccessfully to hold back a smile.

"Come on, you wouldn't have that silly suppressed smile on your face if nothing much happened."

"Well, it was interesting. I noticed there was a beautifully large cumulonimbus stacking up a few miles to the east of Stapleton airport when we landed."

"Uh huh, and what happened *after* the cloud watching," said Sharon, rolling her eyes and giving him "The Look."

After that, John could hardly contain himself. He started behaving like a little kid describing a new toy. He bubbled all over and couldn't sit still. "You really need to see the facility there. It's absolutely beautiful! The communication hook-ups all come into a room on the south side of the reception area and there is ample space for maps and charts. There's a smaller room for receiving computer data direct from the National Weather Service, with compiled information reports for the last 150 years. Their research database goes back over 2,500 years! They've got information pipes from everywhere through a connection to the Global Telecommunications System of the World Weather Watch."

"Okay, what's that?"

"It's a network of weather information constantly coming in from all over the world, from D.C., Moscow, Tokyo, Bangkok, Buenos Aires, Casablanca, Australia, even from satellites, I mean literally everywhere. It's near instantaneous global information sharing!"

John continued his crowing. "Frank says we could probably get a house in Littleton and the station would pay for a computer connection there, too. That way I could receive information and prepare reports at any time, day or night, and even do some broadcasts right from the house."

Sharon thought John was about to hyperventilate and float away. "Wait, wait, slow down. Who's Frank?"

"Frank is the GM at the station, a great guy. He's mainly just interested in cash flow and balance sheets, but I think you'll like him anyway. He gave me two round trip tickets back there for next Saturday. There's of course no obligation, but he really wants to meet you next week."

"Wait a minute, you were just there one day."

"Right, just one day, and now Frank's going to pick us both up at the airport next Saturday, show us the station, and is throwing a luncheon barbecue so we can meet other members of the staff."

John's eyes kind of rolled back in his head for a minute. "You should see the clouds there in Colorado, Sharon. It's like nothing around L.A., the clear blue skies canopy the earth in the daytime across a combination of rolling plains and Rocky Mountains. At night when you stand atop the mountains you can see the stars twinkling as if they go on forever."

"They do go on forever, don't they?" shrugged Sharon,

pulling stray strands of her long dark hair back from her face and smiling at him. "But you didn't see any stars and you didn't stand on any mountain. You were only there one day."

"Where's your imagination," he said, grabbing his bag and heading toward the exit. "The stars go on forever, and even when you've not seen them they're still beautiful, just like you!"

Sharon knew they were both sunk deep into this hook. She went along happily that next Saturday. She liked Frank, and so right after graduation they up and moved to Denver. John's always dreamed of professional role as a weather forecaster had officially been launched.

His other dreamed of role as a father was launched soon thereafter, when little Natalie Wayment was born at Rose Medical Center on the 17th of September 1973.

******

Scott Watson was a diligent student of the weather as well. In addition to ending up designated as a Distinguished Military Graduate he'd finished third in his R.O.T.C. class. While John and Sharon had chosen happily to leave L.A., Scott decided to stay longer at the university to work on a master's degree to better augment his bachelor's degree in meteorology.

For a while Scott felt he was doomed to be a perpetual student. His chosen field of graduate study was the rapidly developing science of weather modification procedures. His master's thesis dealt with the systematized evaluation of the use of carbon dioxide and iodine sulfates in polar air masses with humidity levels between thirty-five and forty percent during winter months around the Oregon and Washington State border.

Unbeknownst to him a copy of that thesis would make its way to The Bunker. It was an innocuous enough subject, but it garnered some unusual interest that would eventually flip everything inside out and change Scott's world forever. That wasn't necessarily unusual since flipping things around seemed to be what Scott was always trying to do anyway. He lived for adventure. He just didn't know this particular adventure might cost him his life, and those of John and Sharon Wayment as well. That fear would come later, but for now Scott was just focused on getting out of school and finding his next adventure.

After graduation Scott had been commissioned as a United States Army officer. He selected the Signal Corps as his branch assignment, which had its principal headquarters at Fort Monmouth, New Jersey. Scott's selection of Signal Corps had been encouraged by Colonel Shelly, Commander of the R.O.T.C. Unit, after he'd received an unusual message directly from the Pentagon congratulating him about his exceptional graduating class, particularly Cadet Watson, and directing him to encourage Cadet Watson and perhaps any others at the top of his class to select the Signal Corps. Colonel Shelly didn't think much about the message and Scott Watson never knew about it.

Scott's Mom proudly pinned the Lieutenant bars on each shoulder at his commissioning ceremony. It was hard for him to maintain proper military bearing and not crack a smile. Others would throw their hats gleefully into the air, but for Scott this was a serious fulfillment of a lifelong dream. He would keep his hat. The Sergeant Major from the university teaching staff came over after the ceremony and demanded money.

"Congratulations sir," said the Sergeant Major, standing at

rigid attention in front of him and holding a salute in long standing Army tradition. "It would be appropriate, sir, for you to now return my salute and pay me one dollar please."

"Imagine that," Scott thought, "I finally achieved my dream. This is the greatest day of my life! Well, maybe the greatest day of my life, so far. Let's hope for a few more still to come that will be even greater." Scott came quickly to attention and returned the courtesy. "Thank you, Sergeant, and please allow me to express my formal appreciation for your excellent training."

"Thank you, sir," the Sergeant winked, "but just the dollar will do." The exchange of smiles then and look of mutual respect was enough for both.

After completing his master's degree, Scott was assigned immediately to active duty, with assignment to the Signal Officer's Basic Course at Fort Gordon, Georgia. He was there only three months before he received his first permanent duty assignment, to headquarters at Fort Monmouth. He had to look on a map to locate Fort Monmouth in the north-central area of New Jersey, just southeast of Red Bank.

Scott caught a military flight from Georgia to McGuire Air Force Base. From there he transferred to Fort Dix and got ground transportation to Fort Monmouth. After he reported for duty the next morning he received orders directing him to an off-site building located six miles south of Red Bank. The building was six stories high, had no name or number, and required special security clearance for entrance.

It was there where Scott really began to blossom and fully embrace this new chapter of adventure in his life. As the weeks and months ticked away to form years, he enjoyed his time spent in that unmarked building more and more. The building wasn't on any military post and he usually didn't have to wear his uniform, which was cool with him.

He could never talk with anyone about the things he was working on, however. Everything was so damned top secret. He thought this was pretty cool, too, but also found it highly annoying. At times he wondered if just the fact he even existed was classified. Ha! It wasn't really the military life he'd expected when he'd signed up, but he loved it anyway.

It was only four years later when Scott received a special field assignment to go to Washington State. He was assigned as liaison officer to the Army Corps of Engineers under Colonel Snow, operating just along the Oregon border, near the active volcanic region of Mount St. Helens.

New Jersey, January 1972

In the summer the wealthy play on the beach at Sea Bright. They pack swimsuits and fly to the Bahamas, Palm Beach, and Coral Gables for the winter. Meanwhile, in the dead blue-black of New York and New Jersey, the wind howls in the ears of those who remain. The ground doesn't just freeze there. It hardens like steel as powdered frost blows about everywhere, stacking along the walks. It whooshes in through cracks to wedge icicles, pierce ears, numb fingers and toes, and jab the heart. Winter arrives with a vengeance, and it seems summer will never come.

As George Radkin drove down Rumson Road toward work that morning, icy wind rocked the car. Even the sound from the radio blew cold as his car's tires clung uncertainly to the frigid roadway. He turned the volume up and heard faintly in the background a small drum beat beginning to build with the arrival of light and flight. "Come with us to the sun," sang the voices. Eastern Airlines had great ads. Listening to the ad, George felt like pulling back on the wheel to lift the car and head south on the wings of the sun.

His mind may have wandered south, but his body remained north. Through the daydream he found himself pulling into the frozen parking lot at The Bunker and exchanging his car for his desk. Sitting at his desk inside his office it was warmer than being out in the car, but the desk didn't have any wings, either. George sighed. After his fingers unthawed around a hot mug of office coffee, he picked up his morning briefing and started to read.

The Atlantic waters east of the Continental Shelf were exceptionally warm. At the same time, reports were coming in that waters around Greenland were exceptionally cold. His staff had written in all capital letters that this unusual combination of cold and warm waters colliding had created "NEAR PERFECT CONDITIONS FOR THE SECOND TEST."

The polar jet stream was strong and currently flowing far to the north. Associated with these exceptional conditions came an extraordinary harvest of icebergs. Actually, it was the greatest number recorded in the North Atlantic since 1912, the year the ocean liner Titanic had sunk on its maiden voyage. If that jet stream could be enhanced and redirected with measurable results, this would prove out their second test, Operation Titanic. What a magnificent name for a disaster.

As predicted, the resultant airflow modification and pattern changes caused from the Operation Titanic field test created a strong sustaining zigzag in the polar jet-stream. This zigzag also forced its flow further south across western Russia on the far side of the globe, pulling along bone-dry air for months.

The success of Operation Titanic caused a drought across Russia and helped push up international food commodity prices, contributing to the Russian grain harvest failure of 1972. This was the intended plan all along, of course, but even the best laid plans can also have unintended consequences. The Kremlin ended up buying one-fourth of the U.S. wheat harvest that year. The massive grain purchases became known as the "Great Soviet Grain Robbery." Farm prices, and consequentially U.S. consumer food prices, shot upward.

The modified, jet stream zigzag that brought drought to the Soviet Union also brought colder, wet weather to the British Isles and eastern United States. The summer of 1972 was dismal.

In June an unintended low-pressure area sucked in Hurricane
Agnes, the most disastrous and costly single storm in American
recorded history up to that time. It rampaged first across Cuba,
then on June 19th slammed ashore in Florida.

Local meteorologists tracked Agnes closely, temporarily
breathing a collective sigh of relief when the wind speeds began to
diminish over South Carolina and she was officially downgraded
from hurricane to tropical storm. She then zigged out to sea, only
to regain strength and zag back hard with even more fury through
Maryland, Virginia, Pennsylvania, New York and New Jersey. The
James River crested in Richmond at thirty-six feet, six feet higher
than the old 1771 record. Fires ravaged streets of homes in
Harrisburg and the governor's 2.4-million-dollar mansion was
filled with water to the first-floor ceiling. More than a hundred
deaths were reported across the region and more than two billion
dollars in property damage.

In Washington, D.C., the Army Corps of Engineers placed
sandbags near the Washington Monument as the Potomac River
surged more than six feet above flood stage, overflowing around
the Kennedy Center for the Performing Arts. One woman driving
fast, trying to escape along a flood-covered road, suddenly found
her car struck by an eight-foot wave. The car was washed
downstream and pinned against a tree in the deluge. Her children
perished, seat-belted to oblivion in the flood-filled steel coffin on
wheels. The woman survived to weep for months as the country
struggled to respond.

When the water subsided, some people prayed and
thanked God for the blessing of still being alive. Some cursed God.
Some cursed the federal government for causing the disaster in the

first place and then for failure to provide adequate aid thereafter.

One particularly outspoken farmer from Franklin County, Pennsylvania, representing what was known as the Tri-State Natural Weather Association, publicly called out recurrent cloud-seeding from the government Project STORMFURY as the primary reason the hurricane had deviated from its natural path. He stated loudly that because Congress appropriated money for such morally-wrong weather control programs as STORMFURY, that Agnes constituted not an act of God, insomuch as it was an act of Congress.

President Nixon declared New York, Pennsylvania, and Virginia federal disaster areas and petitioned Congress for a hundred-million-dollar relief fund. The Senate immediately appropriated twice that amount.

"Follow the money."

–Attributed to Deep Throat,
All The President's Men

Oklahoma, August 1972

There wasn't much there, just a state highway going through from east to west and back again across Northeastern Oklahoma. There was the lake front store with a small cafe and a few rooms for rent in the back, where Harry lived.

Harry operated the cafe and the boat marina. His brother ran the service station and the store. The family had been there since Harry's grandfather settled in as a farmer. Back then it was still part of the great land rush.

Oklahoma is something to be proud of and to defend, all its counties, each with slightly different kinds of laws and peoples. These people love the earth and the ground. They love where they live, the land, the water, Will Rogers, and the government projects that build and maintain the dams and the lakes. They're called Sooners. That's their history, their independence, their families, and their country. The language there has a kind of twill to it. It's not a drawl like Texas. It is unique. Any Sooner can recognize it, and it sounds like home.

On any quiet summer afternoon sitting on a chair overlooking the lake, the gnats fly around. You learn to blow a slight breeze from your lips. With the bottom lip lapped slightly up and over the top, you can blow a quick stream of gnat-removing air, directed alternately at each eye when needed.

That afternoon Harry just didn't understand what was going on when Mario showed up knocking at the door of his home. Mario had been in the cafe and the store before. He'd helped him launch his boat out on the lake several times. Mario had told him this lake was the perfect getaway place. It was a long way from almost anywhere, yet it had a state highway running directly through it. The local Sheriff was never around. He had his own things going on.

Harry really didn't understand, though. Today Mario was there on personal business. It was a long drive down from Kansas City. He was tired and had to get this thing settled. It just wasn't good for the family business to leave loose ends.

"Hi Harry, where's the family?"

"No one's here right now. What's up?"

"Vince and I are traveling through on business to Fort Smith. I want to go look at another piece of property out on the lake. Can you help us?"

It was a slow day and he'd just closed up the cafe. No one else was around. Vince had checked the place out before they came in to be sure of that. Harry's wife had gone into town, and they had waited until Harry had walked down to his home. He usually went home for about one hour or so each day around two, in between lunch and dinner.

The home wasn't much. It was just a small two-bedroom house about a mile down the road from where Harry's grandfather had first started farming.

"We could use your opinion and you know this area. We can give you a lift out there. It'll only take about half an hour."

Mario could see Harry's hesitation, but he knew Harry was always the kind wanting to help out a customer, even though today Harry just didn't understand.

"Sure, I guess so."

On the drive over Mario talked about a piece of land out on the lake that was apparently for sale, but he wasn't interested in the land. He was interested in Harry's cafe and the back rooms. He was interested in money and couldn't comprehend why Harry had turned down a sure thing.

Harry and Mario sat together in the rear seat as the automobile turned south off the state highway. You could get to the lake by going in almost any direction. The lake wrapped around everything in the area, but south was good enough today.

Vince was driving. He never smiled and didn't say much. Vince was a huge guy who sweat a lot in the Oklahoma summer. The air conditioner was blowing on full, but it wasn't helping. Vince had grown huge without any help. Nobody knew for sure his last name. Possibly his mother did, but she never told him. He was simply called Vince, and Vince had now grown into a ruddy, acne-scarred face connected to a 260-pound body, with a twenty-three-inch neck in between. He looked like a football lineman, the kind of guy one could imagine playing for the Bears, the Soviet Union Moscow Bears. Anywhere within ten feet of him there was always a strange odor of sweat mixed with hair tonic and jock itch.

"Vince tells me you turned our offer down. I don't think you understand. There's a lot of money in this for you, Harry. We've already got the feed set up from Hot Springs and it's been running for some weeks. Every day we lose more time. We've got to get our operation set up. We could have our people here tomorrow if you'd simply let us handle things."

Oklahoma was a dry state until 1958. Liquor by the drink was still prohibited, but this depended upon a lot of technical things and what county you were in. Bootleggers and associated corruption were still abundant. Harry had heard about the kinds of businesses that Mario was involved in and didn't want anything to do with it.

"We're doing okay. Janice is in her second year now at Tulsa. Little Jerry will actually graduate from High School next year. We have a good life here. That sort of thing you're talking about, you know I just can't do."

Vince pulled the car around a right turn, drove down the dirt road about a mile, and stopped up on top of a hill. The hill dropped away steeply on one side down to the water with about two hundred feet to the bottom. The dam had backed up the water to here only a few years before, and the brush at the bottom of the lake would be a tangled mass.

Mario opened the left passenger door and got out. Harry hesitated but then got out on the right.

"Look, all we have right now are two girls. They are used to operating on their own and are real professionals. All you will have to do is keep the books. We would install the telephone lines and it won't cost you a thing. All we need is your place to operate from."

Vince had gone to the trunk, taken a large seven-inch flat blade screwdriver out and was working at the right rear wheel. It looked like he was picking rocks out of the tire tread.

"I can't do it, Mario. It isn't about the money. I just don't want it. Besides..." Harry looked away, saying nothing more. He sensed Mario already knew that he'd spoken with the FBI after they had approached him at the cafe last week. He hadn't told them anything, though. There wasn't anything really to tell. He simply wasn't interested.

"Well, damn Harry, no hard feelings. Let's just be friends." He put out his hand to shake with Harry and at the same time nodded to Vince. Mario needed to calm the situation. The last thing Mario needed was some damned informant.

In a minute it was all over.

Mario and Harry were standing near the rear of the car. As they shook hands Vince stood up and motioned for Harry to come over.

"Hey, I think I picked up a nail. Do ya know how to get this tire off?"

Harry walked over and placed his left hand on the rear fender, bending over to look at the tire. With one quick motion Vince's right hand swept forward and up. It was almost silent. The point of the screwdriver glanced off the bridge of Harry's nose, slitting a one-inch gouge and sliding slickly into the socket of his right eye. It buried in about an inch and a quarter before it struck bone at the back of his eye socket.

Harry moaned as he straightened up, grappling with both hands toward his face. As he rose Vince placed his own left hand behind Harry's head and jammed the handle of the screwdriver with his right, driving the shank right through the sphenoid bone, sinking the shaft through the brain, and severing the cells of the basal ganglia.

There wasn't much blood. Harry twitched for a second or two as he crumpled to the ground. Then they just wrapped him up and rolled him over the edge. The chains would catch on the mass of brush at the bottom.

Vince used a handkerchief from his left pocket to wipe his hands as he got back into the car, and they drove away. Mario sat in front with him and didn't say anything. It was just business.

Colorado, November 1979

Frank Fitzsimmons, KWGN-TV General Manager, was pleased. His station's ratings had climbed each year since John Wayment had joined his staff. He lived and breathed by ratings, and for the first time they were now rated number one in local news and weather reporting.

Frank was an excellent manager with exceptional natural ability. He endlessly reviewed reports, polls, and studies about what people wanted to see. His personal objective was to head up a national news media network. He had a vision and obsession with the future and prepared himself for the time he could move away and really take charge. He didn't care to which network he would move. He just wanted to run one of them.

John and Sharon would occasionally talk with each other about how Frank was manipulative, motivated only by money and ratings. He was a climber and that didn't quite fit Sharon's perception of the way things should be, but she remained pleasant and encouraging whenever talking with him at a reception, Chamber of Commerce social, or community event. After John Junior was born, she thought her life was on a perfect track. She had no sense of any danger. She felt comfortable and safe.

After just five years in Colorado, John had become a rather popular local media attraction for KWGN-TV. He'd written a book on weather generation factors and climatic conditions in the Rocky Mountains and Colorado area. It wasn't found on any best seller list, but his obvious dedication and enthusiasm for his work came across strongly in the book and across the airwaves to thousands. He prepared numerous video and slide presentations and spoke in almost every Denver-area elementary school. He was often photographed sitting on the floor with children moving blocks and books around to explain how prevailing winds, ocean currents, upper-air flow, and jet streams worked.

In the basement of the Wayment home was a double-walled room encased by acoustic sound-absorbing material. From that room John gave broadcasts, live and direct, to radio and television affiliates. There were billboards and radio and television commercials advertising his shows. He spent hours in that room. He had installed computer systems, communications links, plotting-graph equipment, and had years of research cataloged within a long row of bookshelves and filing cabinets. Local, regional, national, and global weather maps hung on the walls. It was like a military command nerve center. It was his personal control hub.

John had been collecting decades of historical weather data through many different global intelligence-gathering networks. He had subscribed to all the major weather information services available through ITT, RCA, and Western Union. He had developed his own, custom-predictive software program, to which he was continually improving. The program compared and analyzed millions of possibilities to determine predictable patterns of events. It analyzed possible correlations between rainfall and earthquakes, dust and air temperatures, sunspots and equatorial cloud formations, volcanic eruptions and jet stream flows.

If John's research and programs could more accurately identify changing weather patterns, then the science of weather forecasting would take a giant step forward, enabling him to more accurately predict the future. Achieving this goal was an insatiable hunger buried deep down within his subconscious.

One night in mid-November of 1979, John found himself again sequestered away in his basement sanctuary, hours after dinner, reviewing the latest weekly and monthly comparison reports. He'd been cramming vast amounts of historical severe weather information into his head in the hope of identifying ways to improve his forecasting. He hadn't been sleeping right in months and this kind of study is how he tried to relax himself. In actuality, the increasing number of late nights were just bringing him nightmares, leaving him still stressed out and tired.

While reading through the latest reports on that particular night, however, his mind inexplicably got caught up into prior airflow patterns following major disasters, and the past ten years of his collected singular-event data started speeding forward in his head like a movie. It was in full Technicolor in his mind's eye. Hurricane winds blew, earthquakes convulsed, ocean currents swelled, and volcanoes erupted as he visualized them, with all the patterns and jet stream variations following exactly the sequences he'd been suspecting, except for after a few very particular major events.

The 1973 volcanic eruption of Tyatya in the Kuril Islands of the Soviet Union, just north of Japan, had caused a much larger than expected dust veil. Cooler, dryer conditions across the region had lingered for two years, only to worsen further following the subsequent eruption of Tolbachik, further north in the Kamchatka peninsula. In the United States there were Hurricanes Agnes, Eloise, Kathleen, and now Hurricane David, which had just recently devastated the newly independent nation of Dominica, and many other of the Lesser Antilles islands. Yet then it mysteriously lost its strength and spared Florida and Georgia of any significant damage.

John quickly grabbed his tape recorder, turned it on, and began speaking into the microphone as rapidly as he could, describing everything he saw in his head before the memory was gone. He didn't remember how long he'd kept talking.

Sharon had gone to sleep hours earlier. When she awoke to the alarm clock at 5:00 AM, John was not in his usual place beside her. She found him still in the basement room, mumbling and twisting, slumped over his desk holding his tape recorder. A large pile of notes, maps, and sketches were sprawled out all over the desk and floor.

As she reached out to touch his arm and arouse him, a flash of consciousness burst within John's head. He jerked upright, striking his elbow on the corner of the desk. "Ouch! Dammit, what was that?" Sweat was beading down his neck. He'd been hearing screams inside his head. He'd seen storms and famine and starvation. The terror of his nightmare filled the room.

"Are you okay?" asked Sharon, stepping back quickly. "Was it another nightmare?"

John stood up cradling his elbow and mumbled something like, "I'm not sure…No, I don't think so…I mean *yes*, yes it was!"

"It probably was just a nightmare, but it sure felt real. It was like I was standing on a mountain top weather watching. Then there was an explosion and suddenly I'm watching people die all across the world." John's arm had gone to sleep, and he started shaking it.

"I was working on tracing those severe weather patterns I'd told you about to find their likely future progressions. I think I can finally understand how they intertwine, how they fit together sequentially. At least I think I see now where the common trigger points are and where the consequences from each should naturally emerge. The problem is in many cases they are not. Something unnatural is happening and the consequences are going to be unavoidable." The fear and sweat evaporated slowly as John's blood began to properly return to his extremities again.

The consequences of the increasingly severe weather disasters that he'd studied, read about, watched, and dreamed about were certainly real enough, but the truly personal living nightmare for John and Sharon Wayment had only just begun.

"There's one issue that will define the contours of this century more dramatically than any other, and that is the urgent and growing threat of a changing climate…

No nation is immune. In America, the past decade has been our hottest on record. Along our eastern coast, the city of Miami now floods at high tide. In our west, wildfire season now stretches most of the year. In our heartland, farms have been parched by the worst drought in generations and drenched by the wettest spring in our history. A hurricane left parts of this great city dark and underwater. Some nations already live with far worse. Worldwide, this summer was the hottest ever recorded -- with global carbon emissions still on the rise."

–President Barack Obama, addressing the U.N. Climate Change Summit in New York City, September 23, 2014

At 10:30 hours on November 15, 1979, only flag officers were present in The Bunker conference room. Victor Sine handed a briefing packet to each person as they entered the room then welcomed everyone with his usual security speech. The material was for use only during this meeting, blah, blah, and no one was to take anything from the room.

Each of the packets was boldly marked, "CONDOR NORTH – Top Secret, Eyes Only." Everyone's anticipation felt heightened as George Radkin walked around the room slowly, taking extra time to shake each person's hand and emphasize the significance of the occasion. Once everyone was in their seats, he called the meeting rather solemnly to order and deferred to Admiral Wainsmith first on the agenda.

"All of our test compilations have shown conclusively that modifying the polar jet-stream flow can be accomplished within our expected parameters, through the anticipated cooling of the surrounding air temperature gradients following infusion of the chemical particulate matter," stated the Admiral proudly.

He continued his pontification. "All our atmospheric tracking systems are presently within operational standards. Timing of the release of the chemical matter into the air stream need only be within a degree plus or minus five percent. Our full compilation of the timing factors as they are related to the eruption, the allowance for various air pressure variables, and expected modified jet-stream flow is located behind tab E in your packets."

Everyone else in the room except Sine and Radkin was now shuffling through their packet, looking for tab E. "All the validation sequences were conducted independently at our restricted northern facility at Moffett. The aerospace analysis equipment there is state of the art and allowed us to create perfectly the necessarily exacting test conditions." The Admiral was clearly proud of the Navy's operation there at Moffett Field, just south of San Francisco.

"We used the large low velocity wind tunnel for final determination tests of modified jet-stream air flow using variables between fifty and 350 miles per hour. That tunnel is large enough to accommodate full size airframes. It's more than 200 feet in diameter, actually taller than it is wide, so we can artificially create our own weather systems there. We ran several tests using each of the small to medium sized aircraft that might be used for the release. High velocity air flow tests were made in the adjacent, smaller facilities."

Sine asked his usual question of the Admiral while gesturing around the room. "Would you please summarize for the group the specific security measures that were taken during your final testing operations?"

The Admiral straightened his posture. "Well, the entire area at Moffett Field maintains the tightest security procedures, of course. It is enclosed by a ten-foot patrolled and alarmed fence. Access to each building is controlled by coded time-stamped passes and restricted only to the limited personnel currently assigned there."

He paused to glance across at Sine for approval, who just stared back silently at him, so Wainsmith cleared his throat and continued. "Separate assignments were given to each of the various air-flow research teams. It's highly unlikely any testing or evaluation team member could determine the nature and purpose of the test results without more information than they were individually given because all the teams worked independently. The only place where all of the findings are compiled together is in the packets in front of you."

Referring to the packets the Admiral then went on to talk further about how the timed infusion of the appropriate tonnages of particulate matter tested well within the projected parameters. Furthermore, the release, along with the expected heat generated within the explosion, should definitively result in the desired redirection of the jet stream with associated modification to atmospheric fluctuations, all patently within the measurable requirements.

"So, in summary, you'll find all these projections detailed behind tab E. The Department of the Navy is fully satisfied this project may move forward to the implementation stage if so authorized."

"Of course, the Department of the Navy is fully satisfied," thought General Sampson to himself. He shook his head and shifted a little in his chair to avoid eye contact with the Admiral. This guy clearly believes the Navy can do no wrong. Wainsmith's slowly measured words and pompous presentation style always had a way of getting on Sampson's nerves. He kept his head down and continued flipping through the significant stack of pages behind tab E.

Wainsmith kept right on talking. "The critical factor is the timing and precision of the detonation. That detonation has always been the most significant uncertainty. However, from what I'm led to believe recently, it appears there may have been some new accomplishment completed by the Army since our last meeting that might help set us more at ease?”

“Some new accomplishment? What a jerk,” thought Sampson. “You know we got our part exactly right from the beginning, and it’s really the key factor here.”

“General Sampson, you’re next on the agenda.”

Sampson’s wandering mind snapped back to attention. “Yes, of course, George.” He leaned back in his chair and spoke concisely. “As you all know, the Department of the Army was given the key assignment of determining the best means for the triggering device. We actually did more than that. Our determination has been made and the Army’s final recommendation with complete technical specification is located behind tab F.”

Sampson glanced over at Wainsmith to see if he was appropriately impressed. Seeing no reaction at all he reached down and pulled out two padded, black boxes from his briefcase then pushed his chair back as he stood up. From the boxes he removed two vials containing clear liquid, held them up high, and continued.

“This particular substance has the property of being fully adjustable with a median burn rate of over 10,000 feet per second.” Looking around the table the General waved the vials back and forth so everyone could see them then paused for impact. There was impact. Anyone who knows about explosives should have actually been headed out the door to get themselves at least a half mile away immediately.

“Of course, the substances are harmless until combined, and these particular vials contain only water. Yet the actual substances are both colorless liquids like this.” There was a collective and audible slow exhale around the room.

"Hmm," said Admiral Wainsmith. "I'd understood the Army was still considering a nuclear device or devices."

"Yes, the *suggested* use of nuclear devices was initially considered but has been ruled out for several reasons," said Sampson, almost smiling. "Any thermonuclear device would require a penetration shaft through the subsurface and leave residual radiation, which likely would be detected easily by civilian agencies or actually any individual with the crudest of measuring devices. Even a small device would dramatically raise measurable levels and bring extraordinary attention to the test site, which of course we need to avoid. We will use radioactive isotopes mixed with the liquids for tracking, but there is some naturally occurring radiation associated with volcanic activity that should be sufficient enough to mask this product." General Sampson put the vials back down into the padded boxes.

"Can you tell everyone a little more about the behavior of the liquid?" asked George.

"Many of you might already be familiar with the basic substance," Sampson replied, nodding to George Radkin appreciatively. "Similar liquid explosives have been commonly used in mining operations since original development by DuPont some years ago. The substance will operate within the widest parameters, and the residue has no identifiable signature. As I said, the two liquids are stable as long as they are kept separate. They can be mixed in different proportions in accordance with the tables that are included in your packets."

What General Sampson was announcing was a significant scientific breakthrough, and he knew it. The only place he could talk about it was in this meeting, though, so he wanted to get all the mileage he could out of this presentation. Sampson had enlisted in the Army at seventeen and was commissioned through R.O.T.C. at the University of Nebraska. He had risen quickly through the ranks and was now a respected flag officer, but sometimes he still felt like a lowly and underappreciated Staff Sergeant.

"Our Army labs have been able to advance the use of the product by breaking down the molecular structure and cohesive tension. This latest generation has been tested at the site with penetration of rock strata to a depth of 8,500 feet. Proper injection of the separate liquids into the subsurface fissures will result in a pooling effect of the combined liquids at several levels within the substrata formations. Timing of the detonation can then be controlled by the application of microwave-energized, neutrino subatomic particles, and the proper mixture can be assured through readings from the isotopes. The discovery of how to do this, of course, came along as a direct result of our other ongoing explosives research."

"Thank you, General. I actually wish we could talk more openly and publicly about this." George Radkin stood up as he spoke to the group. "This exceptional scientific breakthrough by the Army here really makes the final implementation of our project possible. Unfortunately, the best we can do is ask General Sampson here today to please extend anonymous appreciation to his staff and colleagues from all of us. This tool not only makes our project possible but brings finesse to the entire operation as well. Thank you again, General."

As Sampson sat down there was only the slightest glimmer of personal pride in his eyes. He knew his presentation had been exceptional. He wanted to get back up to applaud and tell them that the U.S. Army was the best damned service in the best damned country in the world, but he had learned to control his emotions and expressions. Sampson was an excellent card player. "Finesse, ya, finesse," thought General Sampson. "The Army ain't just a big 'ole bunch of dumb shit-eatin' ground pounders. You tell 'em, George." He didn't have to say anything more.

The noise level of the room began to rise. Whispering between a few turned to outright talking between everyone for the next several minutes. The reality was settling in of having finally reached the primary implementation decision point.

"Gentlemen, please, let's continue," said Radkin, bringing the meeting back to order. He held up his packet. "The Department of the Air Force has been conducting overflight sampling above the area for the past five years. Their findings are synopsized behind tab G. A joint Army and Air Force team has been prepared for leading onsite support operations, and the Navy will compile the collected data at Moffett Field for final evaluation."

"Computer projections show the initial detonation series needs to begin two weeks prior to our target date for the primary eruption. Since that primary blast will directly affect a six to eight state area, the expected civilian interest in the eruption should provide sufficient cover for the Army's onsite team, plus the Air Force teams for control and airborne data collection."

Radkin took several blue papers from his case and passed them around the table, one for each person in the room. "Gentlemen, we know natural volcanic activity is increasing in the target area, so time is of the essence. Our mission is to modify this naturally occurring event significantly enough, so our desired final result will be achieved. Air pressure gradients around the location will be within acceptable limits and error factors are also within acceptable levels. All the test results support these final points as our conclusion:

1. Modification of the polar jet stream through adjusting the appropriate pressure gradients can be predicted with reasonable certainty.

2. The airflow mass, by infusion of at least the minimal amount of particulate matter, can be controlled and the projected atmospheric factors determined.

3. The catalytic effect of the explosive material can be timed to produce the infusion of additional particulate material.

4. The expected geologic event as modified will cause the jet stream to shift, resulting in the predicted reduction of the selected atmospheric temperature gradients.

5. Following the initial eruption, stimulating the desired molecular stratospheric levels can be accomplished through the radio-telescope ionization intersection as indicated. The modifications needed to the New Mexico disk antenna field array are in place and the operational software is onsite and secured.

6. Our recognizance team is in place and the initial deployment team can be onsite and operational in two days. A contingency team has been identified and either team is prepared to remain deployed for a protracted time at the site should controlling a second or third eruption be required."

"Excuse me," General Silver interrupted.

"Yes, General Silver?"

"I'm certain it's in our packets, George, but what was finally determined to be the expected yield? Can the particle flow really be sustained over the next three years?"

"The resulting projections are detailed behind tab J, but in short, we expect the cooling and jet-stream shift to stabilize airflow masses into the modified pattern, so there should be at least six to seven years before recovery. You'll find the terrain modification areas and level of impact over time graphed in the material behind tab H."

"The bottom line here today is that we expect increased precipitation and lowering of temperatures throughout the United States and Western Europe, with drought conditions sustained across most areas of the Soviet Union."

George stepped over to a world map hung on the wall and used a pointer. "The Ural Mountains have a similar effect to the jet-stream flow there as the Rocky Mountains do here. There are a lot of variables and substantial uncertainty when projecting several years into the future, but our CIA projections of Soviet food production capabilities for the years following the event leads us to conclude their continuing military buildup capability will not be sustainable. Their economy must necessarily shift to a primary food production and acquisition basis, so we expect them to turn to the international market seeking massive purchases of grain and food commodities. Funds that the Soviets receive through international trade, such as the European Trans-Siberian oil pipeline, must then be spent on food acquisition rather than on their military. The delay in building of that oil pipeline is an essential part of the overall plan as well. That delay is being accomplished, but we're not sure for how long we can maintain

it. "What were the final projections for damage to U.S. properties?"

"Substantial flooding in the central rivers can be expected. Movement of some fixed assets and property there simply cannot be accomplished, so there will be losses. We expect damage along the rivers to be severe, but still well within defined, acceptable parameters. Early warning will be given, and the usual precautions taken."

George then took several draft news releases from his packet and held them up. "There will be scientific stories circulated within the media over the next few years that a routine cycle of minor ice-ages is occurring. The conclusions will be supported and encouraged by existing government reports, and new research grants will be given for universities to develop additional data to support the conclusions."

George set the papers down, took a sip of water, then continued.

"Many communities of people will be required to adjust after this event, but the Soviets will definitely find their economy suffering the most. We fully expect development of at least some of their emerging military systems will end up being sacrificed. Our European allies have already been informed to expect long term adjustment in Soviet internal affairs and are making preparations to be able to have teams deployed for cover operations, if this becomes necessary and appropriate. A unit of the Army Corps of Engineers has already been dispatched to the control test site area and our man put on notice. Major Scott Watson has been with this project since 1975. His assistance, as you all already know, has been invaluable. We have the utmost confidence in his sense of security and national pride. He's been directed to report to Colonel Snow, but the Colonel will receive sealed orders to accommodate his command for Major Watson. Colonel Snow will make all public presentations and direct the men in his command to comply in accordance with the plans and directives in Major Watson's possession. This essentially will place Watson in charge of the site operations."

Sliding his file toward the center of the table, Radkin concluded his remarks. "Under our operational directives your decision is now required for implementation. We're ready to move forward immediately upon your authorization. As soon as onsite activity begins an order will be issued to evacuate civilians from a hundred square-mile area."

Further discussion ensued. Many years of preparations had been required and everyone present had anticipated the day when implementation could begin. After the meeting adjourned Sine had his secretary bring in the champagne.

Within the hour Major Scott Watson was headed for the airport on his way to Portland, carrying with him the sealed orders for primary implementation of Condor North.

Later that night a targeted microwave beam was swept across The Bunker and the big, beautiful clock hanging on the conference-room wall hummed.

Sharon helped John to the guest bedroom where he dropped without another sound. He was exhausted. John never slept past five and it was already nearly six in the morning. The morning weather analysis had to be compiled and announced before commuters hit the streets. She knew what to do. She called the station to notify them that John was ill and unable to work today. Backup wheels were in motion, so John could rest.

It wasn't until nearly 1:30 that afternoon when John began to stir, jolting upright again, wondering where he was and what had happened. How did he get into the guest bed? The last thing he remembered was hurting his elbow on the desk, talking with Sharon, and then closing his eyes for just a minute to think more clearly. Then he remembered the unnatural patterns after certain disastrous events and almost leaped back into his office.

He pushed rewind on his tape deck and waited, waited longer, then pressed play. He reviewed his scrawled notes while he started to listen to last night's recording and saw the same sequence of events coming back to him, plainly replaying in his mind. "It finally makes sense how these events are related!" he exclaimed aloud. Now his job would be to put all these notes together and write everything out. Then he noticed the time. It was two o'clock.

The basement room had no windows. It was impossible to tell if it was two in the morning or two in the afternoon. He turned and ran up the stairs, hitting three at a time.

"Sharon! Sharon! Where is everybody?" It was bright. "I'm late!"

Sharon was in the small bedroom putting John Junior

down for a nap. She came out of the room and closed the door behind her, motioning for quiet.

John stopped abruptly and whispered this time. "I'm late."

"I know, I already took care of it. I told them you were sick and wouldn't be in today. You were exhausted. The receptionist told me it was about damn time."

They both laughed quietly.

"Tell me again, what were you working on last night?"

"The greatest thing. I think I've found it."

"Found what?"

"How the future predictive patterns work in concert with each other. Last night as I was reviewing the usual monthly reports it hit me, kind of like a dream. It was late. Anyway, I can see how they all fit together and there are common trigger points after certain major weather events. I could picture the whole globe turning inside my head, as if I were looking at it from a satellite. All the air currents, clouds, ocean movements, earthquakes, and eruptions over the past ten years that I've been tracking were playing out in sequence."

"So, you're sitting in a dream watching this world weather movie like an astronaut?"

"Well, you could say it was something like that, but then an even more amazing thing happened. While I was watching this movie playing out in my head, I could see how the sequence should continue into the future. I could actually see what was coming next, extending months, or what might even be years into the future."

John was giddy. "I've got to double-check all the figures, of course, but last night the entire thing fell into place. I think I'm beginning to understand where past weather patterns have been altered and how more strongly developing trigger points might project themselves logically forward. Mankind has been *modifying the weather!*"

Sharon looked quizzical, beginning to think John perhaps had finally lost his mind.

"I'm okay, Sharon. It all fits into patterns," his voice raising. "The whole global climate is changing dramatically, but these changes can be foreseen and predicted. It's all interconnected, especially unnatural modifications because of human behavior and influences. Weather patterns are no longer following only sequences of naturally occurring events."

Sharon interrupted, holding her finger to her lips. "The children are napping. You were up late last night. I think you need to rest today."

"I can't rest. Let me show you."

They both went downstairs and for the next hour John described the historical charts, the supporting geologic data, and the sequence of significant severe-weather events up to the present time. There were several pressure points which had led directly to dramatic disasters. Then he showed her the imminent future possibilities. New pressure points were clearly emerging. Depending on how any of these played out he felt he could accurately plot in sequence the likely consequences, and they were not encouraging.

"Overall, global temperatures are increasingly warming at the surface and lower parts of the atmosphere, while cooling in the upper atmosphere. See each of these layers within the atmosphere, Sharon? Increasing heat at the surface and within the ocean is enhancing the power of the polar jet stream and equatorial currents above. If these temperature trends continue to escalate, the climate repercussions in coming years are going to be dramatic and swift."

"There will be heavier snow fall both early and late in the seasons. Some areas will get drenched, while other areas will get parched. There will be a sharp increase in hurricanes, earthquakes, and other natural disasters. Some economies may not be able to rebuild and survive. It's so much clearer to me now how these weather patterns are inextricably linked. We're moving into some dangerous times ahead in many parts of the world."

Fortunately, Sharon was familiar with John's work, so she began to see what he was talking about. Then she began to believe him and understand. That surprised her.

"What will we do? How can you explain this to people who know nothing about it?"

"That's what I do all day, remember? I'll need time to work up some graphs for making a presentation to Frank. If everything checks out in the computer simulations, I'm going to be able to make accurate predictions from these weather patterns over months, maybe even years into the future. Predicting the weather that far into the future has never been done before, not from any scientific approach. Everyone believes weather prediction beyond a few days is impossible to do with any accuracy locally, let alone around the world."

Sharon smiled, "What about Poor Richard's Almanac and stuff like that?"

Even with her smile John still took the comment seriously. "Oh, that was just old Ben Franklin talking about seasonal changes. People relied on aphorisms until they worked

harder and knew better. You know, there's no gains without pains.
Can you call the station again and tell them I won't be in for at
least another week? I actually don't think I'll be able to get back in
there until the week after Thanksgiving."

"Okay, but you've never missed that many days before.
They'll probably believe you're about to die if I just tell them
you're sick. What should I say?"

"Tell them I'm working on a special project that will
require several days of research and field work. They'll understand
that. Besides, it's true."

Sharon made the appropriate phone call, and John set to
his task. Frank called back later saying whatever John was working
on had better be good. After a brief discussion to reassure Frank,
John went back to his reports to determine the validity of what
he'd suspected. He had to know if the key triggers he'd seen and
resulting jet-stream shifts were really artificially influenced and
also if there were really going to be imminent and unavoidable
climate changes coming, or if this bleak future vision was merely a
result of his exhaustion.

John started in with a deeper analysis of chronological
geologic events. He reviewed all his earthquake and volcanic
eruption reports. The timing, strength, and sequence of each
significant eruption were clearly independent air flow trigger
points.

Sharon brought his dinner downstairs to him.

Mount Agung, the big volcano located in the Indonesian
paradise island of Bali, made famous in the musical South Pacific,
erupted violently in March of 1963. Fine dust and sulfurous vapors
were flung into the stratosphere, caught up by high-altitude wind

flows then carried around the world. Magnificent sunsets reddened the tropical sky because of the multitude of minute dust particles lodged in the air, typically fifty millionths of an inch in size.

The ash spread out around the poles, and by intercepting sunlight, cooled the whole world. Carrying into 1964 and 1965, the average temperatures at the earth's surface were measurably reduced, while up at 70,000 feet above the tropical Atlantic Ocean the dust caused the atmosphere to become three degrees warmer.

The explosion of Mount Agung was the biggest single volcanic eruption of the century, with its several subsequent smaller eruptions and pyroclastic flows lasting almost a year. Estimates were made that its dust veil was around eighty percent of the notorious historical eruption of Krakatoa in 1883, which killed more than 36,000 people. Krakatoa is in the southern hemisphere, but its eruption affected weather patterns around the whole world. It became the standard from which all other volcanic eruptions were measured.

John tracked carefully how every giant volcanic eruption affected the global weather patterns for years afterward, until all the very fine dust particles could dissipate. Eruptions of Martinique's Mount Pele in 1902 and Alaska's Katmai volcano in 1912 each reduced the measured intensity of the sun's heat by more than twenty percent. He then tracked how the most violent earthquakes and volcanic eruptions were linked together. The earthquakes occurred in clumps rather than as isolated events then often escalated up in power with disastrous results.

In the one hundred years from 1750 to 1849, the peak of the Little Ice Age, John calculated no fewer than ten dust veils greater than Krakatoa's, including three enormous ones from

Mayon in the Philippines (1766), Tambora in Indonesia (1815), and Coseguina in Nicaragua (1835).

During the years immediately following Tambora's explosion almost everyone on the planet went hungry. Entire harvests perished and were washed away by flooding rains. It was during the atrociously wet summer of 1816 in Switzerland when Lord Byron got depressed to the point where he suggested to Mary Shelly she should write a story, which became the origin of Frankenstein's monster.

It took John a solid week of tracking historical natural disasters and consequent weather patterns, then running follow-up analysis, before he was able to sleep at night for a solid eight hours. His days were quiet, interspersed with trips to the library and not-so-quiet family time, including a raucous Thanksgiving dinner with neighbors and watching of various football games here and there.

By the end of the following week John was able to complete enough of his analysis to conclude with almost certainty that what he'd foreseen was accurate. He ran all the key proofs through his computer programs, some of them twice, and the modeling held true.

The earthquakes and subsequent trigger patterns he'd predicted were there. Everything lined up in sequence, indicating definitively that when carried forward, a new volcanic eruption in the Pacific Northwest would soon be inevitable, and it was likely going to be a big one, bigger than people suspected. That particular eruption, depending on its timing and ultimate severity, was going to modify the polar jet-stream flow. The only question was by how much and for how long. If that jet-stream shift happened in the way he feared it might, and if all the atmospheric temperature trends he'd been tracking continued along the same trajectory, there were going to be truly catastrophic global weather consequences coming for years ahead.

"If there's any good news buried within all of this," he thought, sliding himself into bed after midnight again, "It's that I'll be taking on the role of star weather forecaster. This is what I've always dreamed about!" He had the models and methods now to be able to predict the future within global weather patterns more accurately than anyone's ever done before.

As he drifted into his amazing weather stories dream-world again, he could hear the cheering crowds of people encouraging him along. He was going to warn these people about the impending volcanic eruption and the entire sequence of events leading up to it. He needed to do this and do it soon! Also, people will need to understand and appreciate the serious impact of all the coming man-made climate changes. He was, of course, exactly the right person who could explain all of this. He would bet his career and his life upon it.

"Man," I cried, "how ignorant art thou in thy pride of wisdom!"

–from Frankenstein by Mary Shelley

Television stations really begin to hum in the early morning hours. Even at 6:00 AM John couldn't avoid the well-meaning and good-humored questions from office colleagues, constantly interrupting him as he tried to get himself focused back onto his daily work routine while waiting anxiously for Frank to arrive.

"Heard you've been sick. Did you get the flu?"

"Where have ya been? Finally sneak in a vacation without telling anyone?"

"Good thing your wife called in for ya. We all thought you were out on the town with a girl." When one is usually never gone, it's more difficult to explain a sudden absence.

"You look really tired, John. Are the kids keeping you up at night? Did you get beaten with an ugly stick? Did you get lost chasing down your Thanksgiving turkey?"

******

Just after 8:00 AM John walked to the front reception. "Where's Frank today?" he asked.

"Mr. Fitzsimmons is out this morning, but he should be here after lunch. Try stopping in about 1:30. He has an hour open on his schedule then."

The anticipation reminded John of the third grade, when he couldn't wait to check his weather vane each morning to see which way the wind was blowing. Today his enthusiasm was also leaving him wanting to see which way the wind would blow.

At exactly 1:30 he walked over to Frank's office. Frank wasn't there yet, so John lingered around the hallway, trying to act normal. He practiced breathing slowly in and out to suppress his excitement. "Focus on how this will lead to higher advertising rates and improved ratings," thought John. "Promote the money and improved ratings, promote the money and improved ratings." Frank finally showed up about ten minutes later and John pounced.

John used caution and his best diplomacy, moving from one chart to another, carefully letting it all hang out. He stopped just short of telling Frank about the impending volcanic eruption he knew for certain was about to happen.

"What? People will think we're crazy and ratings will drop. Where's the credibility? People don't want to know what will happen with the weather in six months. They want to know if they should pack an umbrella with them to work or not."

"We'll give them that, Frank. We'll also give them more than any other station in the country. This will be the greatest thing since floppy disks!" John knew from Frank's look that he wasn't getting through. His raw enthusiasm without the full context was just leaving Frank cold and uncertain. "I need to shift gears here or lose the entire pitch," thought John. His mouth moved quickly to fill the breach.

"What I am really asking for here is a special presentation, maybe a lead feature in the TV magazine, supplemented with a series of radio spots to promote it. This needs to be separate and apart from our usual weather forecasting. We can sell this as a history piece, a look backward and then forward into the future."

"Now maybe you're onto something with that. Okay, go ahead and take those charts over to the mag section and talk to Ed. See what he has on the schedule and what he can do. Just be sure to show me the final storyboards before going into production. We don't want people to think we've flipped our corks."

"Can I tell Ed this is all your idea, Frank?" John winked. He knew with Frank's blessing he was in the door with Ed for sure.

"Now, that's smart thinking right there," Frank said, smiling back.

******

John was elated. He knew Ed Gwynn would support his idea. Also, Ed had many good contacts within the network. He decided to go catch Ed right after the 6:30 broadcast was over. Ed would have some free time then, and hopefully he'd be relaxed and open to new ideas.

Not only was Ed relaxed and open after seeing John's charts, he was outright enthusiastic, convinced in just about everything John pitched to him. Ed even made suggestions for how the graphics and historical footage of the volcanic activity sequences could be tied together.

Then he made a suggestion that surprised John, even though it shouldn't have. Ed had seen John's work evolving and improving for the six years he'd been at the station, and he knew John was charismatic and well liked.

"Rather than just one shot, let's put you on TV for several. We can storyboard segments for five or six minutes each and give expansion options out to ten or twelve. We might even be able to get the network interested in picking it up as a continuing series. It'll be like coming from NASA's Mission Control Center and you're the flight director, we can call it, 'Weather Control – with John Wayment'. What do ya think?"

"Seriously, Ed? I love it."

The network crew is actually going to be here in Denver next week doing a Bronco's feature called 'Orange Crush'. You and I can go speak with Jim Karras in person. He's supported similar things before. I think he'll probably like this."

******

That night when John got home, he flew up the front porch stairs to find himself suddenly standing in his kitchen. He didn't remember opening the front door. He was speaking much too fast trying to explain things to Sharon. He realized how excited he really was when Sharon told him to sit down, take a breath, and speak slowly.

"They loved it! *I loved it!* Ed said we might even get network to pick it up as a series. This is the greatest thing that's ever happened to me!"

"What about when we got married?"

"Well, ya, I guess you could say that was pretty great, too."

"Always good to keep things in perspective," laughed Sharon.

"Okay, I'll have to work on that."

"Be careful what you wish for.
You may receive it."

–from The Monkey's Paw by W. W. Jacobs
(1902)

Major Scott Watson's flight touched down to Portland International at 09:45, November 17th, 1979. Staff Sergeant Poulson was there to greet him, coming to attention and saluting as he emerged into the gate area. Scott was taken aback for a second. He hadn't been in a uniform for so many years he'd almost forgotten military courtesy. He returned the salute, shook hands with the Sergeant awkwardly, and said something about being glad to meet'cha. "I've been a civilian way too long," Scott thought as they walked down the long hallway toward the baggage claim.

After a short time, they were on their way. They stopped briefly just outside Kelso, Washington around noon to fill up the black Chevrolet with gas and to answer the calls of nature from drinking too much coffee. From there it was about thirty-five more minutes to the Davis River Road turnoff, along Dahlman to State Road 504, then down a couple miles and up a small pebbled drive to Colonel Snow's command camp near Silver Lake.

Colonel Snow's office was in an appropriately olive drab camouflaged semi-trailer. His office walls were covered with operational maps of the western United States and detailed topographical maps of the Northwest.

"Have a seat, Major. It's been a long time."

Settling himself down into a folding metal chair Scott wondered where he'd seen this man before.

"I first met you in Jersey during the first month of your assignment," said Colonel Snow. "It's good to have you with us out here in the field now, young man."

The Colonel appeared to be around forty-eight years old, probably only forty-five.

"The geologic reports are showing movement and instability. My unit received orders here 'bout five weeks ago. We have a seismic outfit with us now and have set up preliminary monitoring. Have the heads back at that Bunker of yours made any final compilation yet?"

"Well, the geologic conditions are moving along the predicted patterns," Scott said to the Colonel. He didn't know exactly how much Snow knew about the project. Condor North had just barely been approved.

"I sure hope we can prevent extensive damage when this thing actually blows. My teams have been working control and evaluation and we're ready for a big one. Brother, when Helens does blow, her whole top could pop off. I just hope we can make it go in the right direction. I guess we'll know in a few months."

Scott suddenly thought the Colonel somehow knew more than he should. Here was Snow telling him something about "making it go in the right direction." Scott didn't even know what Condor North was really about until a little over two weeks ago. He leaned forward, trying to pay closer attention. Hopefully, he still thinks his teams are here to protect civilian property interests.

Scott had been briefed on Colonel Snow's prior assignments before leaving The Bunker. He was a field ops man primarily assigned to information gathering and evaluation, including stints in Bangladesh. There was no reason the Colonel should know a lot about this project.

As Colonel Snow talked on, Scott began to realize the information he was relaying was only coming from the regular Army Corps of Engineers briefings. Snow's unit had previously participated in experiments conducted by the Army under General

Sampson. He knew something about the placing of the explosive liquids, but clearly still believed this was being done to try to limit major damage, so far as possible, to civilian populations. Scott breathed a sigh of relief.

"Colonel, I've brought with me special orders that I understand you can verify by countersign as authentic and valid." Scott opened his briefcase and pulled out a sealed envelope emboldened with the words, "CONDOR NORTH – Top Secret, Eyes Only." There were also additional random groupings of five letters each: OCRHE WQIOP BHNIF WSDXI GNBRD VMXEY."

Snow turned around to a small safe hidden behind his desk, operated the dial and lever, opened the door and produced a small book. He took the envelope from Scott and quickly deciphered the phrase.

"Are we to open this now or later?"

"Now."

Inside the envelope was a packet of pages detailing out contingency orders. The orders were divided into sections titled "Contingency Plan A" through "Contingency Plan F." Each plan outlined specific instructions to be followed in event the order was received. Colonel Snow was to implement the orders under specified situations or upon receipt of certain code. Major Watson was indicated as the appointed liaison through whom the direct orders were to be received from The Bunker.

"Well, this is unusual, a Colonel taking orders from a Major."

"I'm sorry, Colonel, it isn't really meant to be taken in quite that way. This is a truly special assignment. I should be considered a liaison between your command for implementation of the orders I receive. We both will be receiving these orders from the highest level together. New shipments of material and equipment are to be received in accordance with the schedule you already have. Communications security equipment will be received within the next two days. This additional equipment is for reception of direct satellite communications and for encryption and decoding."

Scott paused to see if the Colonel had any initial reservations or questions, then continued. "We're going to need to get everything ready to move as the snow clears. Our first assignment is going to be arrangements for deployment of vehicles, shelters, and support facilities for around 150 personnel. These personnel are going to be stationed at various areas within the test site, under cover as tourists. The assignment of these troops is classified, and every precaution needs to be taken to provide them cover. Some will be arriving in what will appear to be civilian campers, and we'll need to provide transportation to camping areas for others. Communication codes will be changed daily, and all assigned personnel will be given password, countersigns, and comsec equipment. Identification before communication must always be made without compromise."

"Holy hell. Daily code changes, really?"

"There's good reason for all this extra security, Colonel," said Scott calmly, relaying the cover story. "If environmental groups find out their government intends to interfere in any way with this natural phenomenon we could all end up in some silly civilian TV court before a judge who can't get his head out of his own ass and tie our hands for months. I'm sure you're aware of all the various legal and PR nonsense that is going to doom Project

STORMFURY, just because of public complaints about a little bit of cloud seeding. STORMFURY was directly responsible for saving us any significant damage from Hurricane David, yet nobody will believe them. There are teams of environmentalists and activists out there clamoring around and we don't need that kind of crap affecting Condor North. We need to keep our work here absolutely confidential. If all goes well and we maintain our security, then when this mountain finally blows we will have been able to prevent the destruction of probably millions of dollars in property and likely saved many lives in the process as well."

Nothing in what Scott told the Colonel hinted to the true objective of Condor North. He just repeated the cover story since that's all any field personnel were to know. Scott watched for Snow's reaction as he completed the briefing.

Snow agreed, "It's unfortunate it has to be done in this way, but I guess that's life these days. Even a threat to sue and I can see how these preventative actions could be delayed, and this baby we're sittin' on right here for sure ain't gonna wait for a judge."

Scott relaxed. The objective was to modify this natural event, not cause it to happen or prevent it. St. Helens was going to erupt whether the Army was there or not. Snow seemed to understand the broadest purposes at stake, but of course there was more involved than protecting local property interests, much more.

The U.S. military's involvement in modifying the eruption of Mount St. Helens may or may not save any property or lives. The hidden objective was to time the blast to go off at exactly the right moment and under exactly the right conditions in order to obtain maximum effect in changing the weather to our favor, at the expense of the Russians.

Major Scott Watson was a meteorologist and he believed in the significance of what was really trying to be accomplished here. What he didn't know was that Condor North was only one of many other top-secret operations for modifying weather patterns on a global scale. He didn't know yet about Condor South, for example, and he certainly had no idea what was being planned right then in the Kuril Islands and all around the Sea of Okhotsk, either. He didn't even know Okhotsk existed.

The network magazine people arrived in Denver on Monday morning, December 10th, 1979. John Wayment had been preparing to meet them for days and had draft scripts ready for twelve clips. Twelve was twice the number he realistically thought national would actually agree to air, but he anxiously hoped for more and wanted to be able to drop quickly any scripts they might not like.

Ed Gwynn had arranged things, so John could meet the arriving crew at the airport and drive them back to KWGN-TV in the station's van where they were scheduled to start working on the "Orange Crush" football feature. As they were driving John began to talk with Jim Karras about his future weather forecasting vision. Karras was chief of the network lead news team. He listened politely and by the time they arrived at the station, he was actually asking for details about how John collected his data and how he'd come to base his conclusions. All John had time left to say was, "I'll have to show you the data out at my home."

Luggage and equipment were unloaded from the van, and the network crew went right to work. John was disappointed. He wasn't able to connect again with Karras for four more days, until finally the Broncos clip was in the can and Jim and Ed had time for a visit out to John's home in Littleton.

John showed them his basement studio and proudly explained how he got started in meteorology and studying weather patterns. After about forty-five minutes of his usual passionate display, it was obvious Jim was intrigued with John's knowledge and background. He decided right then and there the first segment should feature John himself and highlight his down-home

American lifestyle.

"For a second feature we can bring in world history and major weather and geologic events," said Jim. "You can talk about hurricanes, volcanic activity, earthquakes, and analysis of air and sea currents."

"Second feature?"

"I'm thinking in the first segment we should be talking about you. You know, your family, your setup here at home, and why you decided to become a meteorologist." He nodded to Ed, "It'll make a nice human-interest story as lead." Until that statement Jim really hadn't said very much. Now it was clear John's bait had been cast and Jim was caught. That's when John really started talking.

He talked to Jim and Ed excitedly for the next hour and a half about major geologic events that had contributed to changing global weather patterns. He brought out all the charts and graphs he'd prepared the past few months to explain the patterns he'd discovered. He pointed out how earthquake and fault areas around the Rocky Mountains were similar to those around the Urals in the Soviet Union and described how the air flow pattern over the Himalayas shifts between summer and winter.

John described how he'd plotted out the speed of upper air currents against the rotation of the globe, and how this impacted jet-stream flow around the mid-latitudes. He explained how he'd found connections between major geologic events, the flow of ocean currents, and the polar jet stream. He explained how these had directly resulted in significant famines lasting for decades across India and Ethiopia.

John brought out color graphs and charts he'd made

showing how the North African climate had changed over the centuries, modifying what was once a fertile farm district into a climate that brought the Sahara Desert. He talked about possible dangerous trigger events that led directly to massive natural disasters in Afghanistan and Bangladesh.

Becoming even more interested, Ed interrupted. "We have film taken by crews in many of those disaster areas. We could get clips. Along with satellite photos we can make up a pretty solid B-roll."

John nodded quickly and kept talking about the observable pattern sequences. "What's happened has created a cooling effect in the northern hemisphere caused by alteration of the weather by a series of predictable events. For example, a jet-stream shift led directly to Hurricane Agnes making landfall along the East Coast in 1972. Future weather prediction relies on a multitude of past variables, far more than I think anyone can track by using traditional meteorological methods. I had to write my own computer programs to validate the analysis. There was no other way to adequately test all the equations. It's now almost 1980. In addition to rapidly increasing global population, we're starting to see increased sunspot activity, an increase in extreme temperatures, and an increased number of severe geologic events around the Ring of Fire, with resultant increased instability in the surrounding areas because of accelerated collision of the continental plates."

"Wait a minute," said Jim. "What do you mean by ring of fire?"

"The Ring of Fire is the area of active volcanic activity all around the Pacific Ocean." John turned the globe to show the area around Hawaii. "Kilauea and other volcanoes in Hawaii were created by underwater lava flow over hundreds of thousands of years. They are not part of the Ring of Fire, but located roughly in the center of it, in the middle of the Pacific Plate, which continues to shift across the ocean floor to the northeast across hot spots, where magma rises through the ocean floor. A major hot spot is what created the Hawaiian Islands chain. The reason those islands form a chain is because of the directional shift of that tectonic plate. The hot spot at the ocean floor stays stationary while the surface shifts. An island is then created and moves north along with the shifting ocean floor as a new island of volcanic rock rises to the surface, which is why we end up with the islands strung out along in a row. Plate shifting occurs constantly all around the Ring of Fire, causing fault lines. Shifting along the San Andreas Fault up the Pacific Coast is what contributed to creation of the huge volcanic mountains there like Mount Baker, Mount Rainier, Mount St. Helens, and Mount Hood."

John rolled out a map of the Pacific Northwest, placed a plastic overlay on top, and continued. "See how this particular string of mountains along the Cascadia Volcanic Arc happens to lay right in line with current jet-stream flow? Consequently, as long as that pattern holds, a substantial eruption there is going to cause a shift in the airflow and bring a significant cooling effect. There will be flooding all across the U.S., particularly along the West Coast, and drought rolling into central Asia. We can predict this well in advance. Many climates around the world are going to become significantly different in the coming years."

"Wait a minute," said Jim again. "So what you're saying is the San Andreas isn't really going to cause California to drop suddenly off into the ocean, but increasing earthquakes and volcanic activity along the fault are definitely going to change all of the world's weather systems, and this can be predicted years in advance?"

"Exactly." He then finally laid out his primary case for enabling a more accurate prediction of future weather. "What I am saying is that historical geologic events have occurred that are directly related to current weather patterns. Future geological events can, at least to some extent, be predictable for what comes next, perhaps even modifiable in certain ways to change or even control future weather."

At this point Jim and Ed were fascinated. John continued.

"A period of extreme climate change is coming. In the near-term the creation of additional stratospheric clouds in the northern hemisphere from the increased volcanic activity is going to cause certain temperature drops in North America over at least the next seven years, contributing to increased rainfall in some areas of the globe and decreased rain in others. When the polar jet-stream shifts, the El Niño mid-Pacific phenomenon is going to occur again, leading to further dramatic collision of the continental plates. The earth's surface will then attempt to make adjustment to the changing temperature patterns and nothing will ever really be the same as before. Increased industrial production of carbon dioxide and air pollution is only going to accelerate degradation of the cycle. The next few decades are going to bring more and more global instability, with increasingly severe weather contrasts that are one hundred percent predictable."

Jim Karras was entranced. "We should begin now with some promotional material. We can put together some teasers and have anchors start to create some buzz around the topic. In the first lead we'll show some severe volcanic activity to build interest, then shift to the future of the weather and how it affects you. I'd say the first segment could probably be ready to air within six months. What do you think?"

"That long?" said John. "Can't we start sooner?" He wanted to start that very day.

Karras smiled, "What I like the most about this is your enthusiasm, John. Thank you for that and also for having us over to your home today. This series is going to need some time and attention paid to it and deserves some proper build-up. 'Weather Control – with John Wayment', I really like the sound of that. Let's see how the public reaction goes. We'll start immediately with putting together a pre-production and promo team. We should be ready to start shooting by June. Can you be ready by then, John?"

"You bet. I'm ready whenever you say go."

"Good, let's get this on the air!"

******

When Jim Karras got back to New York he turned the project over to graphics, historical research, and marketing promotion. After a couple months of internal development things were starting to become real. One of the first steps the network did was ask for clips of film and video taken around weather disasters in Bangladesh and during Hurricane Agnes. One of the second was to air the first promos about the new series coming soon with John Wayment.

******

The next morning Victor Sine received an alert message within his daily security wire. When certain requests are made to access certain information, certain national intelligence agencies have monitors in place to generate certain automated messages to interested parties within the government. A national television network had requested use of disaster coverage from Bangladesh and Hurricane Agnes. A weather forecaster in Denver was working with a production crew to create a new TV series to be called "Weather Control," starting with how increased volcanic activity in the Northwest is going to lead to an imminent major eruption, which in turn is going to lead to global weather modification because of shifted mid-latitude stratospheric air currents containing increased carbon dioxide, aerosol, and volcanic dust.

Sine sat up in his chair with his own vision of treason, espionage, and breach of security. No one could possibly know all this. He immediately thought there must be a security breach. Some bastard's leaked classified information!

He picked up his phone and dialed Herb Case, asking for a complete background check on this unknown meteorologist John Wayment. Where did he come from, what did he know, and how did he know it? "I want everything on this guy from the time that sonofabitch was born, *everything!*"

The U.S. Army's Internal Security Domestic Division was a relatively small, highly-classified section organized for developing intelligence files on selected persons of interest living within the United States who might pose a threat to the internal operations and mission of the Army. It was deliberately established to be separate from the FBI and CIA, but to maintain ongoing communications with both agencies.

Some of the Division's major operations included conducting targeted surveillance of possible radical group participants identified during events at Kent State and public protest marches of the Italian-American Civil Rights League in New York City. Certain Congressmen later famously claimed having no knowledge the division ever existed.

Herb Case's assignment within the classified division was to coordinate intelligence communications with the FBI and CIA. It was in that assignment that he came to meet Victor Sine one hot summer Friday afternoon in 1970. It was on the fourth floor of the Old Post Office Building in Washington, D.C.

Every time Case walked into that building he couldn't help but pause for at least a moment to look out with awe into the huge open central court area. It was an impressive structure. There were not many people in the building that day as he rode up the elevator to the fourth floor and walked east to Sine's office. Though a Captain, he usually wore no uniform. The nature of his assignments required that he not draw attention to himself.

Case had come there to Sine's office expecting to discuss new intelligence they'd received regarding operations of the Weather Underground Organization or WUO, known colloquially as the Weathermen. The division had been keeping surveillance on several persons who had leanings toward possible involvement in the radical group.

The Weathermen group derived their name from thinking they knew which way political and societal winds blew. They taught and espoused violence, believing this was necessary in order to affect social and political change. They believed that by use of revolutionary means they could place their members into strategic positions of political power. There was a plan in motion for the Weathermen to try and kidnap a major cabinet level official. Time was of the essence, so Case was surprised when Sine began by talking about something else entirely.

It quickly became obvious this was going to be a very unusual meeting. Sine didn't seem the least bit interested about the probable kidnapping of one of the senior staff members of the President of the United States. He had other things on his mind, bigger things.

"We have been looking with great interest at you," said Sine. He often used the plural, even when talking only about himself. "We'd like to talk about your personal career interests."

"My career interests?" Being curious, Case shrugged and thought "okay, why not," realizing the topic of the meeting was going to be quite different than he expected anyway. "What do you have in mind?"

"Well, for some time now we have been working on development of security operations for a new special sequence of projects and in need of a person to head up the intelligence division. What I am saying is that we may be interested in a person of your background," said Sine with a glint in his eye. "If you're interested I can make arrangements for your transfer to the unit, it's near Fort Monmouth, New Jersey. If you accept this, it will mean an immediate jump to Major. I'm sure we could work well together."

Herb Case slid back in his chair. "Wait a minute, what kind of special projects are you talking about here? What can you tell me about the objectives?"

Case unquestionably saw himself as opportunistic. He'd graduated just five years before from West Point and his first Army Intelligence Corps assignment had been to Saigon. While there he'd picked up the language and customs very quickly, and his personality magnetically attracted the confidence of local contacts, including informants planted deep within the Saigon government. Among higher-ranking U.S. Army staff officers, he came to be known as "Whizzer." No one was surprised when he'd received transfer orders from Saigon to the Pentagon staff office of Internal Security. He was a natural.

"Look," said Sine. "We can't really talk more about this here, but what I can tell you is we have top priority to coordinate this operation at the highest national security levels. What I should do is have you meet and talk with George, George Radkin. He's the project director and new Under Secretary of Defense. Could you be available for travel tomorrow? Believe me, you're going to want to be involved in this."

"Um, sure, I guess so," said Case. "I can cancel tomorrow morning's meetings and make the day free. What the hell."

"Good, it'll be great to have you on board with us."

"Don't jump to conclusions now. This is just fact finding."

******

Herb Case had made the trip up to The Bunker with Vic Sine the next morning. Of course, he decided he liked the prospects of the new special assignment, particularly the automatic promotion to Major, and he made the move up to New Jersey two months later. That had been ten years ago, and now it was time for another very unusual meeting.

The room was tense. Three people were gathered around the big desk in George Radkin's corner office. Vic Sine seemed like a controlled explosion about to detonate. His eyebrows were snarled and almost singed from the heat of fire in his eyes. "So, tell us Herb, who in the hell is this John Wayment guy?"

It hadn't taken long for Herb Case to pull together the preliminary background information. Such checks are standard procedure for his office assistants at The Bunker. The summary contained the usual birth record, statistical synopsis, list of schools attended, employment history, and any negative credit reports or criminal records. In this case, there were none. The report made it sound like John Wayment was a clean all-around American boy.

Sine knew everybody had something dirty on them, though. You just had to dig deeply enough. He viewed everyone as being various lesser reflections of himself, and the way he thought and behaved always meant having something to hide.

"We need to get a complete FBI background report, a full work-up." Sine knew, however, that he couldn't get the FBI to conduct such an inquiry without substantial negative information, or if the person were being considered for a sensitive security position. He didn't have this, so he made it up.

Papers were prepared to indicate Wayment was to be considered for a position with NASA, which required a top-secret security clearance. Sine attached a short report, completely false and fabricated. The report indicated that Wayment was believed to have been associated with the Weathermen Underground at UCLA.

The investigative case on John Wayment commenced that afternoon at the originating FBI field office in Washington D.C. From there the information was transmitted to the field office in Los Angeles. The investigation had been given a priority designation that required a response within one week and wire transmission through secure communications channels.

Special Agent Karl Swan was assigned the case. UCLA

records gave him information on which classes Wayment attended. He also found out he'd joined several school organizations and had been a member of two honorary societies. There was a record from his hometown high school with a transcript of his grades, Iowa Achievement Test results, and SAT entrance scores.

Unexpectedly, Swan found absolutely no information to imply contact with anyone sympathetic with the Weathermen Underground. He'd even called upon a personal contact through a past informant. The informant didn't have any information, nor any recollection of anyone named Wayment. There actually were only a few UCLA professors who still remembered John Wayment. Those who did described John as trustworthy, well prepared, dedicated, and unquestionably honest.

Professor of meteorology Mylon Stevenson remembered John most specifically, describing him as an excellent student who was well motivated by his own personal desire for achievement. He'd said he was one of the most enjoyable students he'd ever had. He recalled there were two students in his class that year whom he'd identified as the best candidates for pursuing advanced degrees. Neither had perfect grade point averages, but both were in the top quartile and the two had been the best of friends since at least the third grade. If a vote had been taken as most likely to succeed, he'd said it would've been a tie between John Wayment and his good friend Scott Watson who had been a member of the R.O.T.C. and who he believed had joined the Army after college.

A short response letter was sent back to the Washington D.C. office summarizing the collected information and reporting that the inquiry about any connections between John Wayment and the Weathermen had been negative. Swan was surprised then to receive an additional request the next day to forward his full dossier of all his notes on both John Wayment and Scott Watson.

******

"We need to be very, very careful here," said Sine, closing the door to his office and gesturing to Case like a wild man. "Get your most trusted man, no, on second thought, go your damned self! I want you to get out west to that station *now* and find out all you can about Scott Watson and his intentions. If this really is the same guy, I want to know who he's been talking with from home." It was almost like a black light was shining from Sine's face. "If he's had any contact whatsoever with Wayment, you need to escort him immediately back here to this office! Do you understand me?"

"Actually," said Sine after pulling himself together a bit, "I need you to go out to Kansas City first. There's someone there I'd like you to fully brief on everything we know so far about these two." Herb Case took the contact information, nodded quickly to confirm he understood, and left the frenzied office as quickly as possible to start making his travel arrangements.

A particularly long and urgent security report was received on Sine's desk that next Monday morning, but he was still so upset about Wayment and Watson that he hardly noticed. At first glance he'd thought it was about the Soviet's latest troop movements in Afghanistan and set it aside, but it was actually a CIA synopsis of increased Russian activity developing in the Pacific Ocean, around the Sea of Okhotsk.

The CIA intelligence report that showed up on Sine's desk that Monday was the first to conclude the Pacific Ocean was about to become ground zero for an entirely new type of conflict. "The Monday Morning Report," as that particular document came to be known later by legal counsel, was formally titled, "Soviet and Eastern Block Development of the North Pacific Ocean and Soviet Far East."

For security reasons Sine decided the full intelligence report was not to be disseminated to staff at The Bunker but had a synopsis report prepared instead.

The report contained three sections:

1. Description of Target Area: describing the region around the Sea of Okhotsk, and the secret Soviet facilities the CIA had identified there so far,

2. Atmospheric and Oceanic Analysis: describing air and ocean current behaviors, and

3. Projections and Conclusions: the four CIA findings of most significance.

*   *   *   *   *   *   *   *   *   *   *

```
        TOP SECRET - Eyes Only
      (Synopsis for Blue Condor)


SOVIET AND EASTERN BLOCK DEVELOPMENT
                OF
THE NORTH PACIFIC OCEAN AND SOVIET FAR EAST


    1. DESCRIPTION OF TARGET AREA
    The primary emphasis of this report is
```

on the Sea of Okhotsk, the Kamchatskaya
Oblast, the Sakhalinskaya Oblast, and the
Kuril Islands. The geographic area is North
and West of Japan, 58 deg. N. Lat., 160 deg.
E. Long. to the area of the port of
Vladivostok. Also included are points within
the Soviet domination east to the Kuril
Islands and the Bering Sea.

The rugged Kamchatka Peninsula,
together with the Kuril Islands, is the only
active volcanic area of the USSR. Kamchatka
possesses some 127 volcanic cones, thirteen
of which are active. The thirty-six main
islands of the Kuril Island Ridge extends
southwest of Kamchatka, linking the
volcanoes to those near Japan within the
northwest quadrant of the Ring of Fire.

Unique ancient geologic development in
the area has resulted in rock formations
exceptional in mineral wealth, containing
coal, gold, silver, tin, and oil. Military
significance of this region, however, lies
in its strategic importance within the
Soviet Far East.

Hokkaido, the northern most island of
Japan, is at the southern terminus and
within visual sight of the Kuril Island
Ridge of the Sakhalinskaya Oblast. United
States diplomatic policy toward Japan and
Korea continues to be to help strengthen
those governments and economies to act as a
hedge to further Soviet advancement and
development in the area.

Both the Japanese Air Self-Defense
Force (JASDF) and U.S. Air Force operate
electronic surveillance equipment and radar
tracking facilities at Wakkanai, on the
northwestern tip of Hokkaido. The U.S. Air
Force also operates radar and intelligence
facilities at Misawa Air Base on the
northern end of Honshu, the main island of
Japan, as well as a VORTAC air navigational

and monitoring station with reconnaissance aircraft on the island of Shemya. The U.S. Navy station in the area is located at Adak.

Major Soviet Command transportation routes out to the Pacific have traditionally been through Vladivostok. Historical attempts of the Soviets to achieve warm water access ports for their Pacific Fleet or maintain open cold ports has caused ongoing tensions.

Five Soviet airfields from which high-performance protective attack aircraft can be launched and controlled currently exist at locations near Petropaviovsk, Sovetskaya Gavan, Dolinsk, and within the Kuril Island Ridge. International air navigational charts for the region state Soviet policy that, "AIRCRAFT INFRINGING ON NON-FREE-FLYING TERRITORY MAY BE FIRED UPON WITHOUT WARNING." In 1978 a Korean Air Lines Boeing 707 passenger plane was forced down after Soviet attack aircraft shot off a wing tip.

A new hardened missile, naval, and atomic submarine base continues in construction at Petropavlovsk and some kind of new classified facility has started construction on the Kuril Islands with protective close response fighter cover being provided from the Soviet base on the island of Iturup.

Recent satellite surveillance and additional spectra analysis of the area has revealed clandestine construction of large underground facilities in Kamchatka, Sakhalin, and on the Kuril Islands of Iturup, Urup, and Simushir, with slight water warming associated both southeast and north of each facility. Although an increase in radiation dissipation has not been measured, the nature of the significant warming of the surrounding ocean areas has led us to the conclusion that the facilities are nuclear powered. Increased volcanic activity along the island chain has also been noted.

2. ATMOSPHERIC AND OCEANIC ANALYSIS

Coastal mountain systems within the Target Area are positioned such that they intercept most landward flow of moist air from the Pacific Ocean, resulting in monsoonal-orographic precipitation within this region. Naturally dominant Pacific Ocean currents cause moderation of both the summer and winter extremes of temperature, limiting the extent of permafrost.

The Oyashio ocean current originates in the Bearing Sea and flows southwest off the Kamchatka Peninsula and the Kuril Islands, entraining the water from the Sea of Okhotsk. It meets the Kuroshio Current at latitudes between 37 and 40 deg. N. These combined currents are commonly referred to in the west as the Japanese Current, which continues flowing east until nearing the west coast of the United States where it combines with the California Current, running predominantly south. The smaller northern mid-Pacific flow maintains the Alaskan and Aleutian Island Currents.

The combination of the Japanese and California extensions south combine into the North Equatorial Current and Equatorial Countercurrent. Disruptions in the Japanese Current and the resultant extensions and countercurrent effect has been associated recently as the primary instigator of the phenomenon referred to commonly as El Niño, previously thought to be associated only with the Southern Oscillation around the southern Pacific and Indian Oceans.

3. PROJECTIONS AND CONCLUSIONS

A. The U.S.S.R. appears to be developing or has already developed undersea atomic power facilities within the Target Area. Completion of these facilities is expected within the early or mid-1980s and their full operation has the potential to permanently warm ocean waters within the region.

B. Ocean warming within the Oyashio and Kuril Island regions by just a few degrees could result in significant modification to the directional flow of the Japanese Current, affecting atmospheric conditions associated with warmer Pacific currents around Soviet port access facilities. Whether or not this effect is one of the primary purposes for the new atomic power facilities cannot yet be concluded.

C. Positioning of the undersea heat sources, i.e., nuclear plant heat discharge, at the lower end of the Kuril Island Ridge could likely cause the Oyashio current to curve northward and not fully mix with the Japanese Current, potentially strengthening the mid-Pacific El Niño phenomenon of elevated ocean current temperatures and resultant moisture-saturated atmospheric conditions.

D. Historically strong El Niño conditions have been associated with dramatically increased hurricanes and flooding in many parts of the world. An increase in powerful El Niño charged storms originating in California could result in flooding and destruction

of agriculture across the United
States, reducing grain harvest
production capabilities by as much
as 20-30 percent.

TOP SECRET - Eyes Only
(Synopsis for Blue Condor)

The private meeting was confirmed for 09:30 hours on Tuesday, March 18th, 1980. Herb Case had never been to Kansas City and never personally met a certified member of the Mafia. He'd made the privileged arrangements through the intelligence division of the FBI Field Office in Kansas City.

He was met at Kansas City International airport at 08:00 hours by Special Agent John Freese and taken directly to the location. It was at an underground warehouse office for a dry-goods wholesale distributor, built within a former horizontal salt-limestone mine by the river, just north of downtown Kansas City. The facility was a huge labyrinth of carved tunnels reaching back miles into the rock.

To land at the enormous airport terminal and be taken directly into this immense underground warehouse caused Case to flash back to his military days at bunkers in Saigon, Long-Bien, Bien-Hoa, and Manila. The tunnels were equally impressive here. Whole trains could fit inside.

The Calabrese Family controlled most of the significant organized criminal activities in the Midwest, from St. Louis all the way to Denver. Mario, the second youngest member of the crime family, had been an FBI contact for the last twenty-four years. Intelligence information had led to the conclusion that Mario was a third-generation product trying to lead the family toward legitimate businesses. The FBI didn't have any information yet on Mario's activities in Oklahoma or Arkansas.

Twenty-four years ago, Mario had completed college in New York and first met John Freese, a fellow student there who was openly aspiring toward a federal law enforcement career.

Mario had been encouraged to develop a friendship with Freese. At that time Freese knew nothing about Mario's family background.

When Freese finally joined the FBI his routine application background check revealed an acquaintance with Mario during college, but the subsequent in-depth investigation revealed no cause for security concerns or other Calabrese family connections for Freese, and he was accepted in New Agents Class Three, which began in October of 1955. He spent his first year on assignment to Chicago, then was transferred to Kansas City where he was specifically asked to renew his old personal connection with Mario Calabrese. Only a few people knew about Freese's assignment and that Mario was listed as CI-58.

In late 1960, through Special Agent Freese, CI-58 had been requested by the CIA to work out details for a hit against Fidel Castro. It was during a time when CIA covert operations were in full swing, but special care was taken on this particular project to not directly involve the U.S. government.

Castro had defeated Fulgencio Batista for control in Cuba and thus had defeated the Mafia power base there. It was well-known that the Batista government had both high-level U.S. government and Mafia connections. Public cover for the planned hit was going to be that the Mafia had eliminated Castro and Havana would thereby be restored as the gambling and vice market Mecca for the U.S. wealthy class that it once was.

Because of security leaks within the project, someone aware of the plan vigorously opposed the clandestine operation on moral grounds. Castro was permitted to live and later went on to export his own clandestine guerrillas across Africa and Central America.

On this day Special Agent Freese escorted Herb Case to his private meeting in one of the back offices within the sprawling underground warehouse, introducing him to Mario as Darrell Barrett. He then left the office, not knowing the nature of the meeting and not wanting to know. Case was to telephone Freese for transportation back to the airport whenever he was finished.

Case had brought with him blind copies of all the background information that was available on both John Wayment and Scott Watson. He handed the papers over to Mario and explained how his department needed direct surveillance and a detailed personal investigation on John Wayment and his family, without any indication the U.S. government was involved.

Blind copies are documents written on non-letterhead, just unmarked plain paper without reference to any agency or persons in government. They are unsigned, with no other copies made, so they cannot be traced, and the generating agency can deny their existence.

Mario would use the code name Marcia in all communications with the assignment lead, Rick Parsons (actually Vic Sine). The project must be completed within two months and he was to report back to Parsons by calling a phone number assigned to a local exchange in Kansas City.

The phone number was a front. It had been programmed to forward the call automatically through two additional switches to Vic Sine's private security line. In this way that number could not be traced, and Sine would never be more to Mario than an electronically disguised voice named Parsons on the other end of the phone.

Discussion of payment for services rendered concluded

the meeting. It was agreed that Mario would have full autonomy to make his own logistical arrangements and select two other men to work with him. He would be paid $16,000, plus reimbursement for any directly related expenses and costs. $8,000 in unmarked cash would be transferred first, one half of the agreed fee. Mario told him where to send the money, then Case telephoned Freese so he could return to the airport and get back to New Jersey to report all of this to Sine before he needed to continue on out to Portland.

The cash transfer would require certain unique procedures for accounting purposes, and Sine had a couple of ways to accomplish this. The way he preferred most was to have a special assignment budget authorized for consultation services to a phantom company which maintained Post Office Box 2163 in Atlantic City. Sine had taken care to set up the phony company under a pseudonym so it couldn't be traced back to him.

Periodically Sine would consult with himself and authorize payment through the phantom company. He had acquired a second P.O. Box in Atlantic City with number 2763 under a different assumed name. Having that number, all he had to do was change one number on the check payment address and the amount would be delivered to the second box. He would then deposit the check at a bank across the street and later transfer the funds to a different account. He'd established accounts at several banks in different names. He usually let the money sit in one of the accounts for several months before withdrawing. It had taken Sine a long time to get all his account details setup and operating smoothly, but over the past several years he'd been able to transfer substantial sums of money through this laundry.

Herb Case first became aware of the Atlantic City post

office boxes when Mario got paid. Sine had instructed Case to pick up a cashier's check from Box 2763, cash it at the bank across the street using the name on the account, then send the cash by Express Mail to wherever Mario wanted it sent. Sine had been hopped up on anger and in a hurry. It's easy to make mistakes when you're angry and in a hurry.

Gambling bookmaking is kind of a twisted art within accounting. No significant gambling operation can operate in a vacuum. Each increased level of betting requires lay-off bets to balance all the way up. If a large number of people are all betting on a particular horse to win, place, or show, the local bookie must buy or place additional bets with other people up the ladder on different horses to balance out the risk. As long as the bookie keeps his books in balance, he can service his clients well and stay in business off the commission fees. If he doesn't, just one large uncovered payoff could put him out of business and, in fact, make a lot of the wrong kind of people very angry.

Early on during the race season of 1970, Willard Crocker made a serious mistake. As the Calabrese contact man at the track at Hot Springs, Arkansas, he was responsible for bookmaking and for getting actionable intelligence out from the track to the family. He'd thought of himself as important and that nothing would work without him.

One day Crocker up and decided that since he was the one at the track who took the information out (no small feat) that he should be entitled to more of the take, so he'd set up a little extra thing going on the side. Although it was small action, people who work only for money can get very greedy. His employer found out nearly immediately, of course, and decided they didn't like the competition.

Two of the brotherhood from Kansas City were assigned to go inform Crocker that his services were no longer needed. He was actually lucky his job was the only thing terminated that day. His notice of termination, however, wasn't written on a pink slip of paper, it was written on his face. He'd had no unemployment compensation or health insurance benefits.

One early morning as he left his girlfriend's apartment, he'd met rather abruptly with a small leather bag of sand slamming hard into his head, just behind his right ear. That was the last thing he remembered, until he regained consciousness and dragged himself out of the swamp and up to the roadway to nurse his broken ribs, his broken face, and a deep pain in his groin. He found himself fifty miles east of Little Rock, completely naked, trying to hitch a ride to the hospital.

He'd owned up to that mistake, but it had taken him nine years to work himself slowly back into the trust of the organization. He never did enjoy the same degree of trust as before he'd "slipped and fell" that morning outside his girlfriend's apartment. Since that day he was referred to within the family as The Crock of Shit, or just plain Crock for short. The name stuck. Mario said he liked the new name because it would never let the man forget where he had been.

For the past few years Crock had been operating as a bagman in Kansas City. He drove a small delivery van, and occasionally, because of contacts he'd developed in the past, he was asked to check out a client's credit. In other words, he independently investigated the client's assets, so the family organization would know how to collect debts if necessary.

Crock didn't follow normal credit union procedures. Crock would simply point out the scars on the left side of his face and it usually was enough, particularly if Vince came along. Vince didn't need to say or do much either. He just stood up and moved over very close to the client, smelling of festered jock itch and behaving as his usual self until the message came across loud and clear. On several occasions small and even medium sized businesses had been signed over without any argument.

******

After the meeting at the underground warehouse, Mario informed Vince and Crock about a new urgent task he had for them and instructed them to get out to Denver as soon as possible. They arrived into Stapleton Airport on the afternoon of March 20th, 1980, which, quite coincidentally, was the same day a magnitude 4.2 earthquake rocked the area around the Cascade Mountain Range further to the west.

The pair didn't know their new surveillance instructions had come from Victor Sine, Chief of Security for the United States Army's top-secret Blue Condor operation, which had, in fact, triggered that earthquake, causing the subsequent "volcano tremors." Mario didn't know this at the time, either. It wouldn't have mattered, though, because they didn't care.

A day after dispatching Vince and Crock, Mario called the designated switchboard phone number to reach Rick Parsons. The number he dialed was directed through the switchboard exchange and rang into a vacant room in Kansas City, a small unfurnished apartment. Well, it really didn't ring there, the line just went directly into the cheese box that had been placed there, where the box's circuitry then automatically forwarded the call to another location.

The number where the call was forwarded couldn't be traced by anyone, not even the telephone company. The only way to trace this cheese box would have been to examine the interior circuits. However, if anyone picked up or tampered with the box a built-in self-destruct mechanism was set to burn out the circuits by overloading the memory so there could be no record of the forwarding number. The name had nothing to do with how the box worked. It was named for what the first such device had looked like when it was discovered by the FBI back in the 1930s.

Mario's call flew through Sine's elaborate phone system setup and rang into a private dedicated line at his secretary's desk.

"Hello, for whom are you calling?"

"Rick Parsons."

"Thank you, one moment please."

"Parsons here, who is calling?"

"This is Marcia, I am calling to confirm the contract and receipt of the first payment. I figured I should call you directly before doing anything further."

"Yes, I'm glad you did," said the computer-modified voice. "The man in question is a potential threat to our operations and we need any information you can find that might help us compromise him to bring him back under control. This is the present plan. I'd like to speak with you regularly, even daily, if necessary. I will let you know if plans need to change.

"There will be two men in Denver tomorrow. I will call you back in two days."

"Good, it's very important we move rapidly on this matter."

"I'll keep my side up. Just keep yours." Then the phone line went dead.

Lt. Col. Herb Case arrived at Condor North HQ at 13:15 hours on 18 March 1980, two days before the initial significant tremor was triggered, and exactly two months before the major event. Sergeant Poulson escorted him directly to Colonel Snow's command shelter.

At that time none of them knew about the microphones hidden inside the shelter, connected to an Uher tape machine. It was a 4400, four-track, five-inch, highly-sensitive, voice-actuated reel-to-reel. The Colonel would later get very angry and upset about finding this hidden tape machine, but at the time he didn't know any such thing was there.

One man assigned to the unit was a civilian, not military. Other than the Colonel many on the project didn't wear uniforms, so nothing seemed unusual. Vic Sine had told the Colonel this man was assigned to his unit to maintain special communications equipment and accounting records required by DOD and DOA, so he needed to report only to Sine. Unknown to the Colonel the man's assignment there was almost exclusively to operate the Uher machine.

Every conversation within the command shelter was to be recorded. Tapes were to be sent daily via air express directly to the personal attention of Vic Sine, who then had them transcribed almost as quickly as they arrived. His personal secretary then went through to delete all nonessential information and prepared indexed booklets for the files.

"Someday everything we are now doing will be studied by scholars. We have a duty to history and history requires that we keep accurate records." At least this is what Sine told her.

Condor North HQ transcript of 18 March 1980 included the following exchange:

Col. Snow: "Come in Case, we have been expecting you. George Radkin had called to let me know you were coming. Everything's going smoothly, and all material receipts have been on schedule so far. I expect you'll be wanting to meet with Watson?

Lt. Col. Case: "Yes, I would."

Snow: "He isn't here right now. He should be here within the hour, though."

Case: "Good. Did you tell him I was expected?

Snow: "No. We barely were able to talk with him about transportation. Is there trouble?"

Case: "I don't think so. He and I just need close coordination on a particular matter and I've some instructions to review with him. How has he been doing?"

Snow: "Good. We're still expecting the main blow in about two months. We have concealed units north along the fault line and south near Swift Reservoir. Red pins on that map there show each location. The yellow are epicenter locations of preliminary events. We have everything ready for Thursday and I've prepared the status report for Radkin."

Case: "Well it's good to be here. History is in the making. Do you have somewhere I can go to review that report?"

Snow: "Go ahead and sit down. You can use my office here. I need to check with my sergeant on some things, so it should be quiet for the next few hours."

Case: "Thank you. Can you please let

me know when Watson arrives?"

(Break in transcription, portions deleted)

The status report contained 285 pages, with the bulk of it consisting of addenda or attachments sectioned "A" through "Q." It outlined the planned monitoring sites, the sequences for how and where the fluid explosives had been injected, and how and when they would be detonated. The entire document was classified Secret, the highest security classification Snow's command was authorized.

Scott Watson arrived to command HQ while Case was still in Colonel Snow's office reviewing the report. He was surprised to see Herb Case sitting there behind Colonel Snow's desk. He was even more surprised to see Case wearing an Army Lieutenant Colonel uniform with Intelligence Corps insignia. He came to attention and saluted. The microphones captured their conversation, too.

(Transcription continues, Condor North HQ)

Major Watson: "Hello, sir. I wasn't expecting to see you here. Have your quarters arrangements been taken care of?"

Lt. Col. Case: "I'm actually not sure yet how long I'll be staying. I've a reservation at a motel in Kelso, so I'm set for the next few nights. I was just reading the status report and seems things are moving along fine. Looks like the U-2 and SR-70 overflight reports have been coming in regularly. The photos look exceptional. Your detonation-effectiveness projections look good as well. What's been your biggest problem so far?"

Watson: "No real problems, sir. We do have some concern about civilians in the area, of course."

Case: "Well, just do the best you can with that. We humans are always going to be random and unpredictable animals. (pause) By the way, have you had any time off to maintain contact with home? We always worry about that, you know. We send somebody out on assignment and they get so caught up in the job they forget about contact with the rest of the world."

Watson: "All is fine. Mail delivery works, and they even have telephones out here...one on every tree." (slight laughter)

Case: "Your hometown is Denver, isn't it, Watson?"

Watson: "No sir, L.A., I've never been to Denver, well, unless you count a connection through the airport."

Case: "Well then, that's fine. Tomorrow I'd like to see all the operations here close up. Can you make those arrangements to take me around?"

Watson: "That would be fine, sir. I trust you will find everything in order. (pause) We can start out from here tomorrow morning and I'll take you to Swift Reservoir." (pause) Will you have time to finish reviewing the report? The field maps are all there, and you can find results of the equipment operations behind Tab L."

Case: "I should be able to finish reviewing it tonight. (Sounds of papers shuffling) I'll be back here at 08:00."

Watson: "Very good then."

Case: "Okay. Say, Major, I'd like to keep this on the QT and see the troops

unannounced. I'll wear civilian clothes the
remainder of my time here. Let's attract as
little attention as possible."

  Watson: "Understood sir, I'll see you
in the morning." (Sounds of persons
exiting.)

  (Transcription continues, Condor North
HQ.)

  Watson: "Smith, get the Sergeant
Major. (Sounds of using the telephone.)
Hello, Sergeant Major. We have a Lt. Col.
Case who has just arrived here, Intelligence
Officer from project HQ in Jersey. He wants
to personally visit all sites starting
tomorrow. (pause) Yes, we'll probably start
at Swift. Make sure everyone's sharp. He'll
be dressed in civies so get that word around
quickly and quietly."

  (End transcription, 18 Mar 80.)

As he later skimmed through the transcripts from that day,
Victor Sine chuckled to himself, muttering dissatisfaction under his
breath. At least this Scott Watson traitor knows how to give cover
for his people, so they have fair warning when inspection's going
down. Such a shame, tsk-tsk. What a waste.

Crock and Vince were in rows twenty-four and forty-eight, respectively as the airplane flared out and touched down hard at Stapleton on the afternoon of March 20, 1980. Crocker had told Vince they would attract too much attention if they sat together. Actually, he knew Vince attracted attention just by being. Plus, he didn't like Vince's smell, and so he wanted him way back in the smoking section.

Crocker told Vince to get the bags while he checked at the rental car desk for keys to a blue Chevy Impala, then they motored south toward Littleton.

Once in the neighborhood it took them only a few minutes to find the address. The Wayment home was tucked back from the road a bit, behind a few trees, one of many long rows of modest one and two-story houses just past a community park where a group of kids were playing on an old airplane shell that had been propped up to work sort of like a jungle gym. They turned the car around further down the block and parked.

Crock happily left Vince in the car as he scoped the surroundings. The crisp, high-altitude air felt good on his scarred face. He pulled his hood up over his head and zipped his jacket all the way up as he made his way down the street. Pushing through a small tangle of bushes, he then positioned himself close alongside of the house. From his new vantage point, he could see right inside through two long, pane windows.

A woman was there, maybe with someone else, but he couldn't tell yet. He played Peeping Tom for a few minutes, just watching her. She was pretty and seemed to kind of flow from room to room, back and forth. She had long dark hair and a tight figure, maybe twenty-five or thirty years old, tops. It was mid-afternoon and there were not too many people around outside. Several ideas started forming in his head as he watched her, but then he remembered that time he'd been thrown down into the swamp and focused his wandering mind back onto the task at hand.

Usually they would watch a house and case out the area for a while before making any sudden moves, but Mario had told them to try to get some kind of personally compromising information about John Wayment as quickly as possible. As soon as he could no longer see the woman through the window, Crock reached up and connected a very low frequency transmitter to the lower corner of the closest window with a small suction cup, then hurried back to the Impala.

That night they paid cash for two rooms at a motel up on Broadway, and for the next few days listened to the bug, watched the house, and watched the neighborhood. They watched for movements of every police car and diagrammed timing of everything else that moved around the neighborhood until they identified a time the following morning when nobody was at home and when they expected they had at least forty minutes before the next police patrol.

The door lock was a common, cheap, commercial type. It could be opened with a lock pick rake almost as fast as with a key. As he closed the door behind him, Crock took a lamp off one of the tables and sat it on the floor in front of the door. This way it would make a noise if anyone came through. Vince was parked just around the corner, and each had a small CB radio, so Vince could also alert him if he saw anyone approaching the home.

Crock wore nondescript clothes, a thin pair of white

cotton gloves and carried a small mesh bag in his back pocket. He could quickly pull the mesh bag over his face in an emergency. A small Minox camera was in his front pocket, and the CB radio was clipped to his belt.

He rifled through all the cabinet doors and drawers in the kitchen and, finding nothing of particular interest, made his way toward the bedrooms. Skipping the children's rooms initially, he moved quickly into the master. On a nightstand he found a recently completed checkbook register, some paper bills, and a few receipts. He stuffed those into his pocket and started opening drawers. Crock thought it best to not make the break-in exceedingly obvious, so he tried not to make a mess, but he couldn't really help himself. Everything was way too organized and tidy in the house.

At the back of the closet, he found a shoebox with several old photos and letters that looked promising. He sat down and started flipping through them. He took out his Minox and started taking pictures of anything that might tell a sordid story, including love notes, phone numbers, and letters. He also took a picture of the bed, of the family photos on the dresser, and of the beds in the children's rooms.

This was taking way too long, though, and nothing was really jumping out at him. Finally, at the back of one drawer behind ladies underclothes he found a diary. Bingo! As he started flipping through the pages a small piece of paper fell out.

THOUGHTS

Feelings of my mind
From slumber awake;

The poem was creased and wrinkled. There was a signature scrawled at the bottom, "Love, John." Damn, if the name had been different then he might have had something significant here. This dude's wife even saves his corny old love poetry in her private diary, thought Crock, finding himself surprisingly a bit jealous now of this John Wayment guy. Sheesh, what a fry.

He slipped the paper back into the diary and shoved it down into his pocket. Satisfied, Crock tried to close up all the drawers and put everything back into its proper place, but he was in a hurry.

When he got back to the car, he told Vince keeping tabs on this guy was going to be easy-peasy. He told him about the lame house but figured surely something in the diary or checkbook would prove useful as leverage. "And when he accepts that party invitation we sent to his office, Sheila will get him good and drunk," said Crock.

"Oh ya, she'll get him comfortable and get him talking for

sure," Vince replied. "So, our only job for now is to capture recordings and wait. Wanna go get a beer?"

At a local bar the two talked quietly about their success so far. Getting a bug into John's work at the television station would be tougher. It was far easier to get caught. Crock would still make a call just to scope things out but planting a bug there would probably be unnecessary. There will be too much noise there anyway, too much confusion, and way too much information to listen to. Maybe they should put another bug into his car though? That should be enough. After this they would just keep monitoring and await further instructions.

Crock was content with all of their efforts. He didn't even realize he'd left the house without ever having gone downstairs.

"There must be some kind of way out of here,
Said the joker to the thief
There's too much confusion
I can't get no relief."

–Bob Dylan, All Along The Watchtower (1967)

There was a transcribed message slip waiting at the Silver Lake command trailer for Lt. Col. Herb Case when he and Major Watson returned from the Swift Reservoir site following the tremor detonation. Of course, it was from Vic Sine. The message contained one word, "Now."

Case knew exactly what it meant and turned to Watson. "Sine wants us back at the office for a few days."

"What's up?"

"Probably some new information he's going to want to go over with us there. But you seem to have everything in order here anyway. I'll go notify the Colonel and get us scheduled on the first flight into Newark tomorrow morning. Can you be ready?"

"Yessir, it'll be good to have a break. Besides, we're still at least a month before anything significant is likely to happen here."

******

When their plane landed Sine had a driver waiting at Newark airport to meet them. Once back at The Bunker, it didn't take long to see that more was up than just a quiet review of new project information.

"Sit down Watson."

Case remained standing by the door.

"I have a report here that says you are acquainted with a Mr. John Wayment," said Sine, holding up the file and slamming the papers down hard on the desk. The crack made Scott jump as he was trying to sit.

"Yes, I do know a John Wayment, if it's the same one

you're talking about."

Sine was now absolutely certain the two had been colluding. "I'm talking about a John Wayment that was a buddy of yours from the third grade all the way through college. Don't get coy with me here! I'm talking about a John Wayment who knows about weather control and has been talking publicly about confidential information that could blow this entire project. I want to know right now how and from where he got that information."

"I'm not really sure what you mean, sir."

"That's it," said Sine, motioning to Case. "I want a polygraph on this man before we go any further. He's not to leave this building without my express permission. Stay with him. I want you standing there holding his hand if he has to take a piss. Someone from CIA is on their way over right now, you get me?"

"Yessir."

Scott Watson said nothing. A direct challenge like that to a person's integrity is never forgotten.

******

The polygraph examination was not completed until after 1:30 AM. The pre-exam questioning took over three hours. Once all of the questions were reviewed, Scott was carefully hooked up to the machine. His respiration, heart rate, and galvanic skin response were plotted on a long sheet, not unlike being autopsied while alive. This particular polygraph operator also used a black box with a hole in one end that slid over Scott's right index finger. The platesmograph contained a small light that sent readings to the machine to measure his blood flow.

"In the last five years, have you ever given classified

information to unauthorized persons? In the last five years, have you had any contact with, or talked at all to John Wayment? Have you ever talked about or mentioned Blue Condor to John Wayment?" The questions kept coming. They were relentless. "Have you told us everything you know about how John Wayment may have received information?"

Interspersed with the subject-relevant questions were certain blanket control questions like, "Have you ever told a lie?" and "Have you ever taken anything that wasn't yours?" Everybody says no to these control questions and the machine will almost always generate a falsehood response. A liar generates a falsehood response to nearly everything.

Finally, the results of the tests were compiled, and the examiner reported a plus twenty-one, which was more than enough to conclude that Scott Watson was being truthful. Sine was confused. After going over the test results twice with the examiner he finally relented, and Case brought Scott back into his office and shut the door behind them.

"Sit down Watson."

Scott sat in the same chair as before but slid it back further from the desk a couple of feet in doing so. Case went over and sat down on the sofa across the room.

"Tell me about you and Wayment."

"Well, there isn't really much to say. We were friends for years growing up, did everything together. He lives in Denver now. He always wanted to be a weather forecaster and landed a job at a television station there after college. I've always thought of him as an honest and decent person. We haven't talked recently, but I still consider him one of my best friends."

"How do you think he got information about our project?"

Getting irritated now, Scott sat forward in his chair, "I don't know. We've already spent hours tonight talking about that. I didn't give any information to him. I didn't give any information to anyone else that I thought might get to him, either. I don't even know how he would've ever received any information."

"Well, I'm sure you will understand why we had to know this first hand to be sure."

"No, I really don't understand, please explain it to me," asked Scott, feeling overly tired and openly annoyed at this point.

"Normally for security reasons I wouldn't tell you anything, but since you've known Wayment for years then just maybe you can be of some assistance," said Sine, softening his demeanor a bit, strangely seeming almost friendly.

"We received information that this guy is putting together a national network television series about weather control. We have the script in hand for the first piece. It covers mainly background about him, but the promo leads for the rest of the series are eerie. He's going to be talking about projecting weather forecasts way into the future based on trigger events." Sine grimaced. "He's going to talk about modified Pacific Ocean currents and specifically about the imminent eruption of St. Helens and how this is going to modify the polar jet-stream. His projections parallel our own research and modification plans. We've got to know where he's getting his information. If he's truly just researching weather patterns on his own, maybe you can talk him out of doing this series. It's going to draw way too much attention that we don't need."

Scott sat silent while Sine kept on thinking aloud. Maybe

he could still use Watson. Perhaps this series could still go away. "Tell him this series could make a fool of him and ruin his reputation. Tell him you can help get him another job in government. Tell him anything Major Watson, we just need to stop this TV series. Would you at least talk with him and find out what he knows?"

"Okay, I can talk to him. Yes, of course. He's a good friend, but I just haven't seen him for several years. What do you want me to do?"

"Okay, this can work, then. Call him first thing and just tell him you're on leave and have a long stopover in Denver. We'll get you a car there, so you can go meet him at his TV station and find out whatever you can. Don't talk with anyone else about this, you hear? Just call me or Case as soon as you're done, okay?"

"I can leave in the morning," said Scott, looking at his watch. "Well, it's already morning now. Never mind, I can just sleep on the plane. I'll need to go shower and change my clothes, though."

"Fine," said Sine. "Look, you've been here half the night. Why don't I send Case along with you out there to Denver?"

"Let me do this alone or not at all, sir," Scott paused. "Please sir, I'm either trusted or not. I don't need a shadow."

"Okay, okay," Sine looked at Case. "We understand how you feel. We have no reason not to have anything but full confidence in you. Case can check out the tape recorder briefcase for you, so you can use that to easily record all your conversations."

Lt. Col. Herb Case nodded in approval as he stood up. He didn't have any reason to distrust Major Scott Watson at all.

They'd been together almost twenty-four hours a day for the last several days. During that time Herb thought they'd gotten along quite well, and he trusted him. No, he didn't have reservations about Watson, but he was now having quite serious doubts about his Chief of Security.

> *"Among competing theories or explanations, all other things being equal, the one with fewer assumptions is to be preferred."*
>
> *–Occam's Razor*

Soon after checking into his hotel room in downtown Denver, Scott Watson called John Wayment's office. He'd deliberately waited until he was at his hotel so that he wouldn't put any unnecessary pressure on John. It was the weekend and he knew John would invite him to come out and stay at his house. He was anxious to catch up with John and Sharon again, but he really didn't want to impose for too long and wished without recourse that the reasons and circumstances were different.

John was at his desk at the television station when his phone rang. "Hello, John? This is Scott, Scott Watson."

"Scott! What are you doing? I'd recognize that voice anywhere, what a pleasant surprise. What's going on? Speak to me, ol' buddy!"

"Well, I'm actually passing through town. I've an assignment here in Denver for a couple of days so, of course, I had to call. Sorry I couldn't give you more advance warning, but you know how last-minute business is."

"Of course, I'm glad you called. You still in the Army? How's it going? You've always been quite the soldier man. I didn't know Denver was on the Army's radar, ha! Are you going out to The Springs, maybe Fort Carson?"

"Yes, I'm still working for the Army, but you'd hardly know it. I'm actually just here in Denver doing similar things to what you've been doing, except I do it for the government."

"Great! So, can we get together? What's your schedule like?"

"Are you able to connect in the morning?" asked Scott. "I'm beat, but I can call you first thing when I'm up."

"That would be good. Call me at home. Wait a minute, where are you staying? Why don't you come out and stay at our house? I'll be home right after the evening news broadcast."

"That would be great, but I've already got this hotel room and totally worn out."

"No worries call me in the morning, then. Just dial weather."

"What's that?"

"I've a new number, just dial W-E-A-T-H-E-R on the telephone. It cost me a bit to get that number, but it's easy to remember!"

"How about that. You never miss a trick. Do you have a weather vane mounted atop your house, too?" They both laughed. True friends always bring back good memories.

"Nah, just a great big satellite dish now! I'll talk with you tomorrow."

******

The next morning the first thing John did was invite Scott over to the house. John had four treasures in his life: Sharon, his daughter Natalie, little John Junior, and his basement office. He wanted Scott to see them all.

John didn't have any Sunday assignment and he called in a couple favors to get coverage at the station for Monday. They spent the entire day together and most of the next hanging out in the basement. They were like two little boys again, playing with their toys. Scott was enjoying their time together so much he totally forgot about the recorder briefcase. It was still in the trunk of the car.

Scott asked cautiously about the TV series John was working on, and how he came up with the idea. John rambled on for hours about it showing him chart after chart, convincing him in the process that he probably could predict future weather patterns more accurately than any forecaster who had ever lived before.

As John shared all his passion for weather tracking just like he did when they were kids, Scott grew more and more satisfied that his hard-working, dedicated friend hadn't stolen any government secrets. John just had so much weather behavior knowledge stuffed into his brain over the years that he couldn't help it when it started to fall out all over the place. He'd stumbled onto the most amazing things to report for his series and was so excited. How was Scott going to convince John to abandon his dream? He knew he couldn't do it even if he tried, and he didn't want to try.

Before Scott left for the airport that afternoon, he said his goodbyes to Sharon and the kids then gave John a great big hug. They embraced like old friends who had not seen each other in years, and who may not see each other again for many years to come. Scott knew he had to say more. He had to warn them.

"John, you're the best friend I've ever had on earth. You take care of yourself, you hear me? You need to be careful."

Looking at his friend John immediately sensed there was more than what Scott had told him, and asked quizzically, "What do you mean?"

"I really wish we had more time and I could tell you more, but you need to know that some of this work you're doing has attracted more national attention than just from the network. While you're working on this TV series you need to be very careful. Be careful what you say and to whom you talk with about your plans. Some rather significant things are developing and there are others who really want to be able to accurately predict the weather just like you do. Some of those people are the jealous type. While you're working on this series, just watch yourself and your family."

"You're not serious? I appreciate your concern, Scott, but you were always one for conspiracy theories and cloak and dagger stuff."

John suddenly felt a chill run down his back. What was this warning from his friend all about? He thought back to what Sharon had noticed at their house the other day after she'd come home from the store. Several things had seemed out of place and she couldn't find their old checkbook. Maybe she was right that someone had been in their house uninvited, and just shortly before Scott had arrived.

"I'm very serious," said Scott, trying to give a reassuring look. "If you see anyone strange watching you or notice anything unusual at all please give me a call. You've got my numbers."

"Okay, I understand and thank you for being honest with me. Somehow, I didn't think you were just passing through town only for a social visit. I'll be careful. I promise. Sharon had actually told me before you arrived that she thinks someone might be watching our house, and maybe even have been inside while we were away. Do you know anything? You really think someone could be watching us?"

"Shit," said Scott, suddenly shaking inside. "Yes, it's more than possible. You need to really watch yourself. Maybe send Sharon and the kids to go stay with friends for a while. Can you do that?"

"We'll be okay, yes, we'll figure something out. Thank you. Get outta here now and have a good flight." They embraced again, "Friends are forever, Scott."

"No matter what, John. No matter what."

Scott drove solemnly back to Stapleton airport, cursing silently to himself all the way. John went back inside to talk with Sharon, though he wasn't sure what he was going to say. There wasn't much time before his scheduled broadcast at the station. He had to leave quickly so that he wouldn't be late.

******

Once at the terminal Scott called Vic Sine from a payphone to give his report. He described John's explanation of how the upcoming national TV series got started and how it was approved for production. In five weeks Wayment was shooting the introduction piece and soon thereafter they were to start taping all the other Weather Control segments in sequence. The whole series would be fully produced and ready before the end of June.

No, he didn't see any possibility of talking Wayment out of proceeding with the broadcasts. It was just too good. It was his dream, what he'd been working toward his whole life. No, he didn't have any recorded conversations, but he talked about what he'd seen in John's basement and about John's passion for weather forecasting. Scott remained deliberately silent about what John had told him about someone breaking and entering their home.

Sine cut the call short, hung up, and called Herb Case into his office. He shut the door behind him, steam seeming to flow out of his head as he talked.

"You wouldn't believe the bullshit I just got stuffed down my ear. He said Wayment came up with all these segment ideas himself. He gave some story about how he'd mapped out the historical graphics, wrote a computer program in his basement, and having an inspired vision for creating more accurate weather forecasting."

Case sat down gingerly as Sine continued his rant. "We can't trust Watson anymore. Herb, I know he's hiding something from me. The only valuable information he gave is that we have until June to stop this guy. He said they'll be doing the shooting then, and the network plans to start airing in October. I need you to call our contact at the network. See what can be done to stop or at least delay that TV series. Maybe we can pay someone off? We do not need this kind of attention right now. We do not need the public and the media to start asking more questions about weather control."

Case noticed Sine's hand had a slight twitch as he pounded the desk repeatedly with each statement. He tried to divert some of the tension by asking a question. "Any word from our surveillance?"

Sine swung back in his chair. "Yes, we have two men gathering information. If we do end up needing to talk sense into Wayment ourselves we should have some leverage to apply more directly if this becomes necessary, but there's absolutely nothing from the further background investigations so far. He cannot have just come up with all this information on his own. There's got to be something we're not finding. Seriously, what kind of guy is this clean?"

"What about on the Russian front? Any new

developments there?" said Case, finding himself now just wanting to change the subject to anything else.

"Right! Those damn dirty Russians, now *they're* the opposite of squeaky clean!" Vic Sine jumped out of his chair like a cannon shot and moved over to the map on the south wall. "They're the absolute devil with their red flag just dripping blood. Monday Morning Report from CIA said their ocean project is only a few years from being operational. We've got to get better information on what they're up to there at the north of Japan. What did you find out about getting new photos of the area?"

"Sources say we can get updated satellite imagery within a few months."

"Satellites in a few months? We can't wait that long. We need something now, dammit. We need close-up photographs with infrared. We need overflight. What happened to the days of those gutty U-2 pilots? Now those were some real men, flying right over the damn Russians without them even knowing. All we do now is fly maneuvers over our own country to see how the pretty flowers are growing."

Sine walked sullenly back over to his desk and collapsed into his chair. "We need some pilots with enough guts to get over there now and gather us some real intelligence. We need to get better information."

Kuril Islands, Sakhalinskaya Oblast, U.S.S.R., April 1980

Construction under a maskirovka umbrella by the Soviet Air Defense command continued at an accelerated rate just south of Poronaysk on Sakhalin, and at Petropavlovsk on Simushir Island. Tensions were high. Maskirovka, or Russian military deception, is intended to establish an element of surprise that is essential to victory.

The strategic location of Simushir made it the key link in the chain. Within the Kuril Islands it is the third mass of significance north of the coast of Japan and links the Soviet project to the ocean through the Oyashio current (Oya meaning parent and shio meaning current).

Underground substrate construction of the huge nuclear plant at Simushir was now nearly eighty percent complete. This plant was not being built to produce electricity, it was designed to produce mass quantities of heat to warm and redirect the Oyashio. Soviet engineers calculated an increase in gradient temperature of four to five degrees there would be enough to raise up the desired mid-Pacific El Niño phenomenon. Full operation was expected by early 1983 with the audacious goal of starting to change all the world's weather.

Absolute secrecy and security were placed over the project. Established military priorities were set to guarantee the exclusion or destruction of any intruder. Several units of fighter interceptor aircraft were assigned to Kamchatka, Sakhalin, and within the Kuril Islands.

******

Major Vasiliy Kazmin's SU-15 Flagon-F lifted early in the morning hours from the runway on Sakhalin Island. He was a consummate professional, constantly aware of the U.S. threat from aircraft armed with nuclear weapons probing and testing Soviet resolve and readiness.

He was old enough to remember many wars. No family that he knew had not mourned. He remembered the deaths of his cousins, of entire families wiped away. He remembered being told of the sacrifice and slaughter of an entire volunteer battalion of Russian women. The special battalion had been ordered to attack German lines head-on, so they did. They fought hard for their lives, their families, and their homes. Machine guns had piled up the bodies, stacked them high, and riddled the remains.

Now there was a precarious peace, maintained only by a continued show of force of arms and machines of death. This is exactly why his country could never back down, why they must press onward in Afghanistan to secure their borders, and why they must always stay watchful and alert.

Vasiliy Kazmin was stationed there in the Eastern region along with many of his comrades to stay vigilant and keep the peace. He must always be ready. The Soviet Union is a nation at arms watchfully on guard against the designs of aggressors. Trust no one. Enemy civilian aircraft may be operating under military command. Absolute protection against every intrusion, civilian or military, was an absolute necessity.

As the pilot of a lone fighter craft Major Kazmin constituted the basic fire and tactical front line of defense in the area around the Sea of Okhotsk. This particular morning, he was flying another series of practice runs. He flew practice sorties regularly, under all kinds of varied conditions.

Reaching altitude, he keyed his radio transmitter, "This is 805. Am executing course 240. Fuel remainder three tons."

"Course 240, roger."

"I am closing on target, am in lock-on. Distance to target is eight kilometers. Missiles armed and ready. Automatic tracking confirmed."

"Roger."

"I have executed launch."

"The target is destroyed."

"I am breaking off attack. Fuel remainder 1,600."

"Roger. Execute course 320 to 10,500 meters."

"Roger. Executing."

Major Kazmin pulled back on the stick and pointed the needle nose of his craft skyward. As he rolled out at 10,500 meters over Sakhalin Island he had no idea that in less than three years after their nuclear operations were fully functional, he would be given a real target that would make international headlines.

That future target would be Korean Airlines flight 007, a Boeing 747-200B with 269 persons on board, commanded by Chun Byung-in, a former major in the Korean Air Force, with first officer Sohn Dong-hui, a former lieutenant colonel.

KE007 would depart from Anchorage and like a giant lumbering bird it would die four hundred miles off course. In a blinding flash of explosion, it would litter the sky with blood. President Ronald Reagan would go on TV to call this event, "one of the most infamous and reprehensible acts of history."

"The target is not responding."

"Now I have to fall back a bit…Say again?"

"I am dropping back…Now I will try rockets."

At 18:25:11 the Soviet pilot would report to his ground controller, "Understood. I am locked on. Target is at eight kilometers…I am closing on the target. I have already switched on." At 18:26 GMT Kazmin would report, "I have executed the launch…Target destroyed."

The blip of KE007 would take three more minutes before disappearing off the Wakkanai radar screens in Japan, indicating the pilots had wrestled hard with the plane before it finally dropped in pieces into the dark waters below.

The weeks after Scott's visit had been incredibly hectic for John and Sharon. John still didn't quite know what to think about Scott's veiled warning as he'd left for the airport, and he couldn't get himself back into any kind of routine again at work. A headhunter had called asking if he'd be interested in changing careers, but he wasn't.

Had his developing series on the weather really attracted the attention of the wrong kinds of people? What does that even mean? What could actually happen, anyway? It was just a TV series. Yet this was his dream. There was less than a month left until production was scheduled to begin, and he was determined not to get distracted or discouraged.

After several days of stress and indecision, Sharon had relented and taken the children to stay with some friends across town for a while. These friends also had children about the same age so it was rather a fun adventure for them, but John was finding himself alone at the house on most evenings now. He found himself getting more and more paranoid, seeing shadows move around outside at night.

That evening John headed home immediately after the ten o'clock news broadcast had ended. He arrived at his usual late hour to find all the lights on and Sharon there waiting for him in the living room. By looking at her face as soon as he walked in the door he knew something was wrong.

While he was on air at the station, John's father had been trying to call him. He'd finally reached Sharon at their friends' house. There had been a helicopter crash in the mountains somewhere near Washington State. Scott Watson had been killed.

There wasn't any additional information, only that there had been an explosion on impact, so he'd likely died instantly without suffering. She had come straight back home so she could be there when he arrived. Yes, the kids were fine and sleeping.

"How is that possible? I don't believe it. He was just sitting here with us a few weeks ago." John slumped down into a chair by the window. Sharon moved over and sat beside him on the ottoman. She didn't say anything. She just sat there with him and gently held his hand.

John couldn't move. He felt frozen. He was thinking back about his friend. "This isn't right. We used to ride our bikes…We did everything together. It's not fair. It's not fair." He rubbed his eyes until they were red, refusing to cry.

Finally, Sharon said, "I think…Probably we should get some rest. We should go to bed."

"Not yet," said John standing up. "I'm going downstairs for a few minutes."

Over the years Sharon had learned that trying to reason with him at times like this didn't do any good. She couldn't change him. She would only try to support and help him as much as possible. "Okay but come to bed as soon as you can. I need you too, John."

John went to his basement retreat and just sat for a while, listening to the silence. He didn't turn on the computer or even pick up a piece of paper. He just sat, thinking. He felt like the weight of a heavy void was crushing him to the floor. Was there something he should do? Anything he could do? There was nothing, just his feelings of the great loss. He prayed for his sanity. He prayed for Scott's family. "O God, please comfort them in their loss."

Then he did reach over and turn on the computer. He didn't do any work on weather analysis or with his television show though. He started writing a memorial to his friend. The words poured themselves out from his soul and he had to capture them.

FRIENDS ARE FOREVER

When I was a boy, I had a friend
The closest friend a boy ever had on earth
We talked like boys, we walked like boys
And flew on bicycles fast like the wind

Through the years we grew closer still
Our voices hushed, winds whistled and rushed
Our clasped hands grew stronger together
We weathered the storms and pounding rains

Now as the winds of time quiet this place
He's still a friend of mine
The race he's won now, my fast friend
Bright stars are aflame, reflecting his fame

He flies through clouds today on full glorious wings
While waiting on high, beyond the veil he sings
Still struggle I here, yet I know my friend is near
I'll quiet my tears to remember back the years

Until we meet up high, our hands to clasp again
In strength and bond of friendship that perseveres
No winds shall blow anymore to hush the sounds
That boys made down low those many years

The next morning John didn't go into the station. He and Sharon sat together at their breakfast table with extra strong coffee and cold cereal for breakfast.

"Huh, what did you say?" John still wasn't quite awake.

"I said you haven't yet taken your boy camping. John Junior is five years old now. We live so close to these beautiful mountains. Let's get out of here for a few days and go camping together."

Snapping himself to better attention John said, "Maybe that's it. We should go camping. There's time before the series starts shooting. Most of the work is already done."

The basement had been turned into a veritable fortress of computer printouts, charts, drawings, graphs, and revised scripts. John had put all this chaos together. Without him the Weather Control series wouldn't be. There was nobody else who could do the job. "Yes, we should get away for a few days. We can plan out every detail."

A master at seizing onto an opportunity, Sharon agreed John had a fine idea. Of course, she would have to make all the specific plans for where to go and what to bring to eat, but she was delighted. They gathered back little Natalie and John Junior from their friends' home that afternoon right after school and headed for the mountains.

In less than two hours, they arrived at the first campsite. Sharon turned the car down a Forest Service road to a parking spot way off from the highway. She pulled up next to a small campfire facility near a picnic table, tucked back within a tall grove of trees.

John estimated the Douglas Fir near the table was at least ninety feet tall. While Natalie worked to discover if she could climb up through the first few branches, Sharon and John opened the trunk and began to pull out the equipment and set up camp. John pitched the tent and stuffed in the sleeping bags and mats.

Sharon gathered the utensils and set out ham and cheese for dinner. After they'd all eaten they walked down a short trail which led to a small stream, then opened up into a beautiful view of a meadow of grass, drying flower stocks, and aspen trees.

John began to explain to Natalie the difference between the Western Coneflower and the Aspen Coneflower. "See the dark brown cylinder-shaped head of this plant?" said John, holding up a stalk of the plant along with a stalk of the Aspen Sunflower. "Can you say Rudbeckia Accidentalis? How about this one. Can you say Helianthella Uniflora?"

"Are we really here to teach Latin?" said Sharon, smiling. Taking him by the hand with a gesture of insistence she walked him and the children over to a soft grassy spot at the edge of the meadow and laid out a blanket. The sun was hanging low on the horizon now. John noticed the light breeze was coming south-southwest at about five knots and the cumulus clouds were moving northeast. He wondered what the barometer reading might be at this altitude.

It was right then when he felt it. He'd forgotten all his stress right there, in that moment. He sat down and noticed for what seemed like the first time the azure blue sky growing darker in the distance over the misty, blue-gray mountains many miles away. He smelled the pine, heard a mockingbird, and saw an eagle floating high above in the sky. He didn't sense anything except the grass, trees, clean smell of the air, and this quiet place with his family. Sharon was watching the children chasing a butterfly.

"Daddy, Daddy, look how pretty red the sky is!"

John knew what they were seeing in the sunset was increased refraction from the extra particulate matter spread throughout the stratosphere from Mount St. Helens having belched on cue. Volcanic dust blown from deep within the earth had mingled with the sun and colored the sky. He felt his eyes close as Sharon lay down next to him and placed her hand gently on his arm.

That night, removed from the city lights and smog, the stars overhead filled the immense sky. The Milky Way arched, supporting the vault of heaven. The stars twinkling that night looked like they could go on forever, but the world would never be the same, not for John or Sharon, or for anyone.

It's the worst thing I have ever seen.
It had been described to me earlier, but it was
much worse than the description had impressed
me...Enormous blocks of ice apparently are still
covered by literally hundreds of feet of fluffy,
face-powder-type ash, and as that ice is melted
under the hot conditions that exist, enormous
cave-ins are taking place. Steam is bubbling up.
There are a few fires about. Someone said it was
like a Moonscape but it's much worse than
anything I've ever seen in pictures of the
Moon's surface.

–President Jimmy Carter, commenting to
reporters following an inspection tour of areas
damaged by the Mount St. Helens eruption,
May 22, 1980.

The cataclysmic explosion of Mount St. Helens occurred on the morning of May 18, 1980.

A second eruption occurred May 25th. Others were still to follow. Each was carefully timed and slightly altered from the injection of the paired liquid explosive, detonated by energizing the neutrino subatomic particles via microwave transmission.

As soon as the data from the initial blast was finally all compiled and evaluated in New Jersey, the project had already been labeled a success. The injection of particulate matter and gaseous constituents had indeed reached above the troposphere and high enough into the stratosphere to be within acceptable parameters.

Thousands of small earthquakes had rocked the region for weeks. Then, in only a few minutes, the initial blast blew away 1,300 feet of mountain, devastated more than 200 square miles all around, and buried Harry R. Truman at the Mount St. Helens Lodge under more than a hundred feet of ashen, gray debris. His body was never recovered. The resulting landslide was the largest debris avalanche in recorded history.

The effort to release the cryptodome bulge sideways along the north-facing side was accomplished. The reach of the primary Plinian column (named for Pliny the Younger, who had described the disastrous eruption of Vesuvius in 79 A.D.) had successfully been modified by more than nine percent, resulting in the intended enhanced impact upon the highest atmospheric conditions.

With some ongoing extra assistance from targeted low-level radio waves the resultant ash cloud spread across the United

States in three days and had circled the Earth in fifteen days, modifying slightly the polar jet stream flow along with it. The officially recorded staff conclusion was that the events triggered from the Mount St. Helens eruption firmly established the base conclusion that "Atmospheric climatological conditions could be meaningfully modified by man on a global scale."

"Everybody talks about the weather, but nobody does anything about it." This oft-quoted statement made by Charles Warner in 1897 was no longer true. Vic Sine thought it typical of people to attribute that statement to Mark Twain, because, well, people were inherently stupid. He preferred to reflect on some of Twain's actual good advice to, "Never argue with stupid people. They will drag you down to their level and then beat you with experience."

On Monday morning of May 26th, the day after the second blast, Vic Sine was in his office reading through the latest field reports. He was finding himself growing even more confident and wondered aloud why hard-working people who actually make things happen never seem to get properly credited. "At least with this project, with all of the detailed records we're keeping, history won't soon forget the name Victor Sine!"

He looked up suddenly and was startled to see Herb Case standing at his door. He smiled wide and called him into his office jubilantly. "We're living in astonishing times here, Case. The world will never be the same!"

Case had brought with him a file. It contained results of additional FBI background checks requested on John Wayment that were conducted in California and Colorado, a letter from their TV network contact, and pages of information from "Marcia" with notes and recordings from Colorado.

As Sine began to read the front synopsis memo his countenance changed almost immediately from exuberant confidence to an ashen, mountain gray. He didn't say a word. He just sat the report down on his desk and closed it.

"That will be all, Case. Close the door on your way out."

He flipped through the contents of the file and read through the synopsis more carefully.

May 26, 1980

To: Victor Sine
       Chief of Security

Fr: Herbert Case
       Deputy Chief of Security

RE: FINAL REPORT - SPECIAL
INVESTIGATION - JOHN WAYMENT

1. The additional FBI background investigations conducted on John Wayment are inconclusive, finding no prior criminal activity, nor any connections to others involved in such.

2. No information or evidence whatsoever has been received to indicate that John Wayment had improper contact with Maj. Scott Watson or any other Army officer, contractor, or other representative related to Blue Condor. Major Watson's applied polygraph test and conclusions from his personal visit corroborates this.

3. Information collected through the Kansas City contact is inconclusive also. Weeks of surveillance with multiple recordings taken at his home and from his

car have revealed nothing significant in
John Wayment's personal or professional
behavior or background that would
substantially imply reason for suspicion of
his having access to any information related
to Blue Condor, or that might be used to try
to compromise him into agreeing to drop
plans for the Weather Control series to air
as planned. He expressed no interest in
speaking with an employment headhunter about
a job change and declined two prearranged
invitations to attend social events without
being in the company of his wife.

    4. Our national television network
contact (SA-5) reports that it is near
impossible to block production of the
Weather Control series. The executives in
charge of the program refuse to cut the
series without receiving substantially more
information as justification. Providing any
additional information would wholly
jeopardize the anonymity and security of the
project. Reachable contacts within the
network have declined several invitations to
accept money to drop the program.

    5. Final production for the Weather
Control series is scheduled to begin at the
network on 15 June. It is estimated that
Weather Control will capture a national
audience in excess of fifty million viewers.

Sine sat immovable and mute for a moment, then reached
for the telephone. Rick Parsons calmly called Marcia. "Yes, I have
all your damned reports in front of me right now, but everything
still shows inconclusive…Certainly we'd hoped to resolve this
problem by other means, but those attempts have failed…Yes,
that's exactly what I'm saying, John Wayment and his family
constitute a present and immediate threat to national security. It is

imperative that the threat be removed prior to June 14th. Will you be able to perform?"

There was a long pause before he resumed. "I'm not interested if you think you can. This arrangement must be certain…Yes, the entire family…Yes, you'll have half in advance and be shielded. Anything that's necessary we'll see is taken care of. Just make damn sure all bases are covered and attract as little attention as possible. Make it look like an accident, or just have them disappear…You do your job and I'll do mine. I'll send you the mail today."

Sine hung up the phone and told his secretary he would be back in two hours. As he walked from his office he complimented himself for having prepared for this contingency well in advance.

Lt. Col. Case's training as an Army Intelligence Officer had taught him to be meticulous. He had learned never to draw conclusions without certain and conclusive evidence. To keep himself balanced he often repeated the mantra, "I know what I measure, not what I see." That training had served him well many times before. Case knew the world was not always as it appeared.

One instructor of his in particular had taught his soldiers well on how to methodically think twice, even three times, before making any significant military intelligence decision.

An aerial photograph was projected on the screen the first day of class, as the teacher challenged the students for answers. The photograph had been taken by a reconnaissance aircraft at 10,000 feet above an open field. A line of trees cut across the north, and there was a large haystack in the center of the field. There appeared to be a pipe, clearly visible, protruding from the south side of the haystack. From the trees there were two parallel track impressions in the earth leading to the haystack.

"What do you have here?" That was the first question.

The obvious response had come immediately from a young soldier on the third row named Herb Case. "A tank. It's a tank camouflaged underneath the hay." Several other students nodded approval, but then immediately he knew they all had been set up.

"Wrong," said the teacher. "What we will learn together this semester is proper methodology for basic intelligence analysis and evaluation. First and foremost, never jump to conclusions."

The teacher picked up a pointer and moved to the screen. "What you have here is a haystack with a pipe sticking out and two parallel tracks between here and the trees. This could be a tank hidden within the haystack, or this could be a decoy. It could also be nothing."

It had taken Case a long time to definitively reach the conclusion that his Chief of Security needed to be watched very carefully and closely. He'd seen Sine staying awake nights at a time, coming to the office very early in the morning and working straight through the day without a break. He had been observed on several occasions quickly switching from a very pleasant personality to one of cold insensitivity and depression. Sine's actions in the last few months had caused his haystack to start rumbling across the field.

Case moved quickly now, trailing Sine carefully at a distance as they both left the building. Sine had full use of a government vehicle, but he didn't go out the side door to the motor pool. He walked out the front door toward the employee parking lot to his private vehicle and headed south on the Garden State Parkway toward Atlantic City.

Sine's orange Porsche 911 was not difficult to follow. Case kept himself at an inconspicuous distance as they exited to downtown. The car finally squealed off Atlantic Avenue and into the Post Office parking lot. Case watched from a distance as Sine first went into the Post Office and then to the bank across the street.

He was in the bank ten minutes, long enough. Sine typically conducted financial transactions by mail, so it was unusual for him to personally go to the bank in the middle of the day. After leaving the bank Sine went again back inside the Post Office. Case was certain now. He turned his car around slowly and headed back toward The Bunker. His suspicions were being confirmed. Sine's haystack was rumbling further across the field, shaking the ground, and large pieces of concealing hay were falling off to reveal an M48 Patton tank underneath.

That evening Sine left the office with most of the employees. There was no urgent new business and Condor North had officially been designated a success. Nobody was staying late tonight, except Case. He stayed until after everyone else had left and the char crew had completed their rounds.

After the building was completely silent Case entered Sine's office through the side door and locked it behind him. He quickly and efficiently looked through and underneath all the desk and credenza drawers, making sure to put everything he moved back into its proper place. He couldn't imagine Sine kept anything secret in his desk. It would be too obvious. He knew, however, that if he could find any private records or receipts, there would be no doubt. Case knew something had to be there. Sine was a total control freak, and he would never breach his own security regulations by taking things home or stashing them in his car.

He methodically checked through the bookshelves and shook each book, but nothing fell out or became obvious. There was nothing behind any of the picture frames, and there didn't appear to be any loose tile in the ceiling. The acoustical tiles had all been glued directly to the plaster.

Then, as he pulled a small drawer out of the lamp table, he heard the faint sound of paper scraping against the wood. He looked at the drawer, top and bottom, but there was nothing. There were only two pencils and a small pad of paper inside. Then he looked at the hole in the table where the drawer had been and saw where Sine had made a mistake. There was a plastic envelope taped inside, underneath the table top, but the old tape wasn't fully stuck to the wood, so it had caught and made the scratching noise when he'd removed the drawer.

Case reached in and detached the envelope. Inside was a small record book. Several names were listed inside the cover with a signature under each. The book had four parts, each part with a different bank name at the top. Within the book he found a receipt for an insured Express Mail package to Kansas City with today's date, May 26, 1980. There were no withdrawals listed for today's date, but Case was not surprised. Large bank deposits and withdrawals can attract attention, so Sine probably had been removing cash a little at a time and stashing into a safe deposit box.

Quickly reading through each of the four account records, Case totaled up that over eighty-five thousand dollars in deposits had gone through the accounts in the last two months. The book showed a current balance of five thousand.

Case went out to the printer room and made photocopies of the book and the Express Mail receipt. He put a small pen mark on the back of both so that he could positively identify the originals if he ever saw them again. Then he placed the envelope back under the table top in the same position as before, closed the drawer, and left the office.

With copies of the Wayment file, his own statements of what he had observed, plus copies of the hidden bank records and the Express Mail receipt, Case knew he could now convince someone else that his fear for Wayment's safety was justified. He still wondered whether or not Sine was operating on his own or under direction, but he didn't have the luxury of taking more time to find out.

It was almost midnight now and he was already halfway home, but he stopped. He turned his car around and instead started driving south toward Washington, D.C. to visit a friend he believed he could trust. In Saigon he had worked closely with Raymond Young, now a liaison officer for the National Security Agency at the White House.

******

The next morning Mario Calabrese received the Express Mail package. He counted the contents, thirty thousand dollars in old bills of mixed serial numbers. Thirty thousand, even without the other half, would still be enough. Mario telephoned Vince and Crock in Colorado.

It was almost time for the ten o'clock Denver evening news broadcast.

"Where's Wayment? We're on in ten. He was here earlier. Where did he go? He's never late. Has anyone heard from him?"

"He checked out at 6:30, probably went over to campus to get something to eat. Don't worry, he's always here. He'll be here."

Six minutes until air time.

"Check those finals on radar. Can someone color the maps with those new blips? We better have it ready when John runs in."

"Don't worry, he's not first up. We've still got ten minutes after the first cue."

Three minutes to air time.

The producer picked up the interoffice telephone and punched reception. "Where's Wayment? Have you seen him come back yet? What's going on? Or maybe I should ask what's not going on. What's not going on is the weather."

"You can't cancel the weather."

"Ha ha, there's no time left for jokes." He threw down the receiver in frustration. "Everybody on set. We'd better tell a clerk to write up a script for the prompter. We'll have the anchors read it."

"Don't worry, he'll be here."

The floor director raised his right hand in counting. For the last five seconds he raised all fingers, putting one down each second: 5, 4, 3, 2, 1. Bending out of view on center camera he pointed to the lead anchor.

The small red light blinked on.

******

Earlier, at about 6:30 that evening, John Wayment had left the studio to get a sandwich. He liked a small place over near the University. He knew he had to be back by 8:15 to prepare the final forecast updates, but there would be plenty of time. He drove out from the station parking lot and turned east. A pair of round-eyed binoculars from a rented, blue Impala parked down the street watched him leave. John didn't know yet that he'd just driven away from the station parking lot for the last time.

After he turned left on Broadway he stopped at the light. He was the first car next to the crosswalk on the inside lane and several pedestrians began to cross in front. One was a large man in a suit who looked rather like a professional football lineman. As the man moved over the crosswalk he glanced quickly at the locking button on the passenger door of John's car and saw that it was up. When John drove alone at night he usually locked the doors, but it wasn't dark yet, or maybe he'd forgotten.

In that split second, the lineman in the crosswalk moved quickly to the passenger side of John's car, opened the door, and slid in next to him.

"Hey! What's going on?"

The man motioned with a finger to his lips for John to be quiet. He pulled government credentials from his suit jacket pocket and displayed them in his outreached hand: Joseph Geary – Treasury. Motioning to the right side of the road he mouthed silently to John the words, *"Pull over here, please."*

Adrenaline had shot through his body as soon as the man had opened the door and now his muscles were completely tense.

He was at full alert. John suddenly remembered Scott Watson's last words to him. He turned right at the next street, pulled over and stopped the car.

The lineman shifted slightly to the left and pushed back the right flap of his coat to reveal a .38 revolver stuffed into a leather holster on his belt. Just barely below a whisper he then mouthed the words, "*Get out.*" A second man emerged from a brown Dodge service van on the right side of the road and swiftly moved across the street to open John's driver's side door.

"Please come with us."

John jerked around, and his voice jumped a full scale upward, "Seriously?"

"I'm afraid we must insist."

John wanted to run, but there was no place to go. The men led him away from his car and toward the van, "Please get in, we have to go *now.*"

Inside the rear of the van was empty except for a wooden storage crate and two bucket seats. As he sat in the left seat and the door was closed John immediately noticed the windows. The windows were all covered with a black canvas fastened with snaps at the edges. Immediately behind the driver's seat there was also a black canvas covering across side-to-side and from floor-to-roof, so he couldn't see forward. It was like the window canvas, secured with snap fasteners on the roof and sides.

The lineman sat in the seat next to John and spoke. "Regulations require that I ask you to fasten your seatbelt." The van started to move.

"The seatbelt? Damn, the seatbelt! I want to know what's going on and I want to know right now," said John, trying unsuccessfully to sound confident and brave.

A voice came from the other side of the canvas in front. "Please don't be upset. We need your cooperation and assure you that you are not going to be harmed. Your life is in danger. We're here to help you."

"Where are we going? Who are you guys?"

"We're from the treasury department and this is a matter of national security. I'm sorry we can't tell you anything more, because, well, we really don't know more. Suffice it to say we have reason to believe your life is in immediate danger and have been told to retrieve and bring you quickly to a place of safety."

All John could do next was sit back and mutter to himself, "Well, this is one hell of a way to make me feel safe."

After a short drive the van stopped, waited, turned left, then bumped over a metal sounding grate. John could hear the sounds of airplanes and feel them heading down a slight incline. Within a few more moments the van stopped again. The back doors opened to reveal they were parked inside an aircraft hangar. There were two small airplanes there, one on each side of the van.

John's two unidentified escorts in suits got out of the van. They waited for him to slowly emerge as well, then guided him up the short set of stairs into the plane parked on the left, a sleek white twin engine Gulfstream II with "United States of America" written in block letters above the windows on the side. The shades on every window were pulled down. As they all sat down inside the plane someone else on the outside closed and secured the door. The engines began to whine to life, first on the right, then on the left. It took only about five minutes until they were moving.

The lineman was sitting in the seat directly next to John

and didn't say anything more during the entire flight. John thought it best not to try to make small talk. They were in the air several hours before John felt the plane slow and he heard the landing-gear hydraulics as the wheels lowered and locked into place.

Where were they? As John stepped down the stairs from the jet he noted the air was at least fifteen degrees cooler than Denver. There was a wind blowing slightly from whatever direction that was.

There was a brown van waiting there similar to the one in Denver, but with two bench seats inside. The windows were covered as before, and the same type of canvas was snapped into place behind the driver's seat from side-to-side and roof-to-floor. He and his escorts assumed their same positions as when he was first picked up. The lineman was never more than three feet from his side.

They drove in silence for another hour or so before they finally stopped. He heard the driver speaking to someone on the outside of the van.

"Go on in. You're cleared through."

It sounded like a rolling steel door was opening, then the van moved ahead and kept driving for a few more minutes. The sound of the tires seemed to be making an echo now. When they all got out of the van, they were inside what looked like some kind of underground cavern or carved mine. John was escorted hurriedly down a side hallway into a small room. There was a metal toilet coming out of the white stone wall on one side, a small bed along the other, two floor lamps, and a side table with a stack of magazines sitting next to a gray lounge chair.

"You'll have to wait here. Don't worry, we'll be back very

soon."

His escorts left him alone in the room and John heard the door lock. He waited.

John felt like an animal caged inside a vault. The walls were all white, made of solid rock. He paced the floor and measured the room, walking heel-to-toe from wall-to-wall twice, each way. It was almost fifteen feet square, but there were no clear corners. The room looked like it had been raw hewn into the stone and then someone painted the walls white and poured concrete on the floor and made it level. It must be concrete. The floor was painted gray and there was a small gray rug next to the bed.

"This whole place must be underground," thought John. Scraping a small bit of paint from one part of the wall near the door he exposed the rock. It appeared to be a diorite or syenite granite, so he surmised he could be inside any mountain nearly anywhere, from California to New York.

The door appeared normal enough. Looking closer and tapping it lightly, John thought it must be steel. The casing was steel, cemented by masonry into the walls. He tried opening the door handle. Nope, it was still locked.

The temperature in the room felt to be about sixty-seven degrees. An underground facility like this should naturally be only about fifty degrees, John supposed. He looked around the room again for ventilation sources. In the block masonry by the door was a steel bar ventilator grill about one-foot square. It was, like the door, cemented in and wouldn't budge. Then he noticed across the room a small electric heating device, anchored to the floor behind the table. It wouldn't budge, either.

This entire time John was continually worried about what might have happened to Sharon and the kids. The lineman had never answered any of his questions except with a grunt and a shoulder shrug. What had he gotten himself into? Why had Scott told him to watch out and be careful? He'd warned John to keep Sharon and the kids safe. That was only shortly before Scott had inexplicably died in the helicopter crash.

John took a piece of paper and pen out of his jacket pocket. He always carried a folded piece of typing paper in his pocket, usually to make notes about the weather. This time he started to write a description of what had happened to him that evening, of whatever he could remember from the time he was picked up. He tried to remember a description of everyone and everything he had seen. He wrote small, but it wasn't much.

About halfway down the paper he stopped and thought, "Department of Treasury? What does the Treasury have to do with anything?" The Treasury ID had looked well enough like an official U.S. Government ID, but then again, John had never seen a Treasury ID. Certainly the jet had been official looking enough. What about the vans? He'd never thought to look for the license plates of the vans. He wrote down a few more observations, then tried to think of different ways he could conceal the note on or about his body, just in case his body should ever be found.

How long had he been in the room? An hour passed, then two, then three. John kept looking at his watch. He moved from the chair and lay down onto the bed. That didn't help. He just couldn't sit still. "I wonder what happened to my broadcast. Fitzsimmons will be livid. What am I going to tell him?"

Then the door opened. It was the lineman, "Come with me. He's ready for you." John joined him apprehensively, but eager to understand why he was there.

They left the room, turned right, and walked deeper into

the cavern down the stone hallway. The walls here were tiled and the ceiling rounded to the sides. It was a long tunnel with fluorescent light fixtures secured under the apex of the arched vault. "For sure this is an official government facility," thought John. "There's almost zero color in this entire place."

Their footsteps echoed as they came to a T in the hallway. They turned left and passed through a set of heavy steel doors John estimated were at least eighteen inches thick, with massive hinges. Eighty paces further they turned right at another intersecting hall which had several doors down each side, spaced about thirty feet apart. The doors looked just like the one on the room in which John had been kept for the past three hours. They stopped at the third door on the right. The lineman opened it and walked through, so John followed.

The interior of the room was bright, thankfully with some actual color and warmth. It looked like any typical office reception area, except there were no windows. To the left was a dark leather sofa and to the right were two high-backed chairs with a lamp on a table in between. A nondescript painting of a mountain scene hung on the wall. In the center was a secretary desk, properly equipped, with a pleasant and polite sounding young lady behind it.

"You may go right in. He's waiting for you." They walked past the secretary and through the next door.

"Good morning Mr. Wayment!" smiled a tall dark man in a white shirt and tie, standing up from behind a large desk. "I'm sorry to have kept you waiting and in the dark. No doubt you found our methods a little abrupt today, but I hope now to be able to answer some of your questions."

"Abrupt?" John's voice shook. It was a relief to hear a

pleasant voice and attitude, but all of the tension and fear John had been containing so well suddenly came out in a rush of emotion.

"I've been kidnapped by force at gun point, thrown into a van, then flown off to some unknown place and held against my will, all without knowing what was going on or why. I don't know where my family is. Nobody has told me anything. Yes, you could say you were a little abrupt.

The man now walked out from behind the desk and extended his hand. "Please, we are friends. Give us a moment to explain."

"I wish you would," said John, ignoring the extended hand.

"Some of the things you have been working on for your new Weather Control series and that you wish to present on TV has attracted more than just the national network's attention. Unfortunately, a couple of days ago one of the people working on a particular operation decided independently that you had become a threat to national security."

"Me? Seriously? A threat to national security?"

"Well, a few months ago certain high-ranking military officials authorized the implementation of an experimental project. I can't tell you much about the project, except that it involved things similar to what you've been promoting for your Weather Control series. The project was theoretical and intended for observational data gathering for research and development purposes. A full-scale execution was never sanctioned."

"You mean a project about predicting the weather?"

"In a sense, yes."

"You said my family was in danger? Are they okay?

Where is my family?"

"Yes, your entire family was in imminent danger and this is why we had to act as fast as we did. As it is, I was only notified about fifteen minutes ago that Sharon, Natalie, and John Junior are all safe. We didn't know how this was going to play out, but we have them in the air and they should be arriving here in a couple of hours."

All the pent-up anger and fear started to rise into John's face again. He flushed red as tears he'd held back for too long started to come uncontrollably. "My family? You know my family? What happened to them? Have they been hurt? What have you done with them?"

"It's okay, John. They're safe now."

"Are you sure you have my family? How do I know? How do I know any part of what you're saying is true?" John kept backing up until he was flat against the wall. He was breathing heavy and sobbing openly now as he tried to wipe his eyes on his sleeve.

"It's really okay. Yes, your family is fine. Please, try to calm down."

"I don't know you! I don't know where I am," he nearly collapsed. "I was brought here by force. What do you want me to say? Are you expecting me to say thank you? Probably I should tell you I want to call my lawyer. Yes, I think I want to call my lawyer right now."

"Okay, okay, I understand, really I do."

"You understand? Well that's so very nice to know! I feel so good, *so* much better already," said John, nearly shouting, shaking with as much sarcasm as he could muster.

"I really can only imagine what you're feeling right now, John, but yes, I do understand." Moving back toward the desk and reaching for the telephone, the man continued, "Just hang in there for me. Let me see what I can do." He started punching buttons on the face of the telephone. After about fifteen seconds he punched some more buttons.

John felt like punching him, or punching the big lineman, or punching the hard rock wall. He just felt like punching anything.

"Yes, this is NSA-3, countersign follows." He then punched six more digits on the phone. "Yes sir. We do have Mr. Wayment here with us right now. Yes sir, that's correct, sir. What's that again, sir? Yes, I understand. You're okay to talk with him now? Yessir, certainly sir." He reached out to hand the telephone receiver to John.

John took it and immediately recognized the distinctive southern voice on the other end of the phone. "Hello, John, this is the President. I'm sure you must be very anxious. That's completely understandable. Let me just say personally that you're in good hands. We're sorry about what you've had to go through today, but please give us some time and I'm sure this will make more sense. I want you to know for certain that your family is on their way to meet you right now."

John's knees were shaking. He couldn't stop them. He recognized President Jimmy Carter's voice. Of course he did, but he was significantly shaken up, feeling stubborn and bull-headed, and overly cautious of everything. He whistled into the phone, then quickly composed himself.

"Mr. President, wow." John straightened himself up, almost like coming to attention. "I mean really wow, I don't mean

to be impolite, but how do I know this is really you? It's possible
for many people to sound like somebody they really aren't."

"Today you're going to have to trust me, John," said the
President calmly. "Look, I'll have the arrangements made to
transfer you and your family out to Camp David tomorrow. It will
be more comfortable there. I'm sorry I won't be able to meet with
you in person, but I guarantee someone else will be there who
you'll definitely want to talk with."

"Yes sir, thank you Mr. President, Sir."

"Everything is going to be alright, John. Now let me talk
to Ray again."

"Ray?"

"Yes, Raymond Young, he's the man who put you on the
phone. He's one of my best liaison officers. You see, this news
about you happened so fast we had to use Treasury, some of my
own Secret Service Agents. I'm sure he'll be able to explain things
better for you if you give him a chance."

After John caught his breath he handed the phone back to
Raymond Young and listened to him intently for the next hour.

When Sharon and the kids arrived the family-reunion was
joyous. The tears this time were completely blissful. They all
followed Ray back into a small but comfortable interior suite of
rooms within the complex where they could eat and get some
much-needed rest. John found himself breathing easier as he
slowly began to believe again that everything really was going to
be alright.

The next day they were all taken in the van back to an
aircraft hangar in which was waiting the same twin-engine
Gulfstream jet that brought John out there to the mysterious carven

fortress. The windows on the van and the airplane were covered as before during the entire trip. They could see nothing of their surroundings and Ray apologized again that he could not permit them to know where they had been, nor should they ever talk about being there, as this was a necessary security precaution. It was okay. They all nodded that they understood.

By this time John was feeling much more comfortable and relaxed. With Sharon again by his side, and the kids strapped safely into the seats next to them, he actually felt more confident and secure than he had since way back before Scott had said those ominous last words to him, warning him to watch himself and be careful. Hearing the devastating news about the helicopter crash and Scott's death seemed like it was an eon ago, but really it had only been about a month.

Now, after his time spent talking with Raymond Young, and of course his impromptu chat with President Carter, John felt he was ready for taking on anything that might come at him. He was prepared. Actually, however, there was no way he could have been adequately prepared by Ray, The President, or anyone else for what was about to happen next.

"We've been cleared to land in D.C. in twenty minutes," said the Air Force Major, coming through the small doorway into the forward portion of the passenger compartment. The Major leaned over an empty seat and pushed up a window blind. "You may open the other blinds now if you wish."

Eagerly the kids went around the plane and slid up all of the window blinds. The forested hills far below looked like the Appalachians. The sun shown in the starboard side and a carpet of soft clouds billowed in the radiant light.

To John the whole world seemed somehow new and reborn. "What a beautiful morning." Small towns, roads, and rivers passed below as the craft began to slow and descend. The feeling of being there in that sleek government jet flying down into Washington D.C. was exhilarating. Ribbons became highways crowded with cars and trucks traveling in opposite directions. The trees grew larger and more distinct, then the curves of the Capital Beltway and the Potomac River appeared, guiding them along before final approach into Andrews.

A long limousine with government plates was there waiting for them. As they deplaned and walked toward the limo John saw the driver get out and open the rear door. His jaw dropped as he saw his father step out.

John rushed forward to embrace him, "Dad, what are you doing here?" Mr. Wayment hugged his boy close as Sharon, Natalie, and John Junior came up. Then John's mother got out of the car. Everyone was squealing with happiness. For a moment there was just one big circle of clasping arms entwined and more tears of joy.

"I don't know when I've ever been happier to see anyone," John said, his arm still firmly around his mother, holding her close. Reunions of loved ones under stress always brings out the deepest of emotions. "I was told Sharon and the kids were coming, but Mom, Dad, how did you get here? How did this happen?"

"It is quite a story," said John's Dad, smiling widely. We actually weren't sure exactly what was going to happen. We're just very glad to see you all safe. Thanks to…" Mr. Wayment caught himself. "Well, you'll need to come see for yourself, I think you'll understand. Mistakes were made the way things went down, but there was just no other way to do this."

"What d'ya mean Dad?"

"You'll see and be able to understand when we get there, I'm sure."

The driver loaded Sharon's bags into the trunk as they all piled into the limousine. The kids climbed up onto Grandpa's and Grandma's laps as the driver wheeled the machine out through the base gate and waved at the guard.

Even though the drive around the Beltway and then up I-270 to Camp David took about an hour and a half, the perpetual talking in the rear seats made the trip seem like it only took minutes. When the driver pulled up to the guard station entrance they were cleared quickly through and drove down a winding roadway into the presidential retreat complex.

"This is quite a place here," said John's Mom excitedly as the limousine swung down a smaller driveway through some pines to a cottage. "They told us this house where you'll stay is the one that was used by Anwar Sadat."

The driver helped them out while Sharon brushed John Junior's hair from his eyes. Mr. Wayment walked in the front door of the cottage first, followed by John. Nothing could've prepared John for the shock as they entered. Rising from a large red chair by the fireplace was Scott Watson.

"Scott? Scott. How?" John's knees buckled. He grabbed for the top of a chair to steady himself. "What happened? Scott! I thought you were gone."

"I'm so sorry we had to do that to you," said Scott, moving forward slowly. "After the threat came against my life we had to make it look as if certain people had been successful. They were tracking you and your family, John. Your house and car were even bugged. We had to be very careful."

John looked pale, as if he would wilt. Sharon did, sliding down into a corner of the sofa.

"To say it's good to see you just isn't sufficient. I just don't know what else to say or even how to act."

"Just get over here and give me a hug then," said Scott, smiling broadly.

They embraced for a long time.

"Tell me, tell me what happened," said John. "Dad? How did you get involved in this? Sharon said you were the one who called to report Scott had been lost."

"Let's take one thing at a time, son. I think Scott should explain."

"Well," said Scott. "Shortly after I left you guys in Denver I discovered the project I was working on had never been authorized for final implementation. It went directly against the U.N. Environmental Modification Convention treaty and there was